Praise for the Night Stalkers series:

"Top 10 Romance of 2012."
– Booklist, *The Night Is Mine*

"Top 5 Romance of 2012."
–NPR, *I Own the Dawn*

"Suzanne Brockmann fans will love this."
–Booklist, *Wait Until Dark*

"Best 5 Romance of 2013."
–Barnes & Noble, *Take Over at Midnight*

"Nominee for Reviewer's Choice Award
for Best Romantic Suspense of 2014."
–RT Book Reviews, *Light Up the Night*

"Score 5 – Reviewer Top Pick – Buchman writes
with unusual sensitivity and delicacy for such a
hard-edged genre."
–Publishers Weekly, *Bring On the Dusk*

The Night Stalkers 5E

Target of the Heart

The Night Stalkers 5E

Target of the Heart

by

M. L. Buchman

Discover more by this author at:
www.mlbuchman.com

Cover images:
Beautiful Passionate Couple Over White Photo
© Photobac | Dreamstime.com
Chinook Flying From Sun Photo
© Anadmist | Dreamstime.com

Buchman Bookworks

Other works by this author:

Romances
-The Night Stalkers-
The Night Is Mine
I Own the Dawn
Daniel's Christmas
Wait Until Dark
Frank's Independence Day
Peter's Christmas
Take Over at Midnight
The Night Stalkers Special Features
Light Up the Night
Chistmas at Steel Beach
Bring On the Dusk

-The Night Stalkers 5E-
Target of the Heart

-Firehawks-
Pure Heat
Wildfire at Dawn
Full Blaze
Wildfire at Larch Creek

-Angelo's Hearth-
Where Dreams Are Born
Where Dreams Reside
Maria's Christmas Table
Where Dreams Unfold
Where Dreams Are Written

Thrillers
Swap Out!
One Chef!
Two Chef!

SF/F
Nara
Monk's Maze

-Dieties Anonymous-
Cookbook from Hell: Reheated
Saviors 101: the first book of the Reluctant Messiah

Chapter 1

*M*ajor *Pete Napier hovered* his MH-47G Chinook
helicopter ten kilometers outside of Lhasa, Tibet and a mere two
inches off the tundra. A mixed action team of Delta Force and
The Activity—the slipperiest intel group on the planet—flung
themselves aboard.

The additional load sent an infinitesimal shift in the cyclic
control in his right hand. The hydraulics to close the rear loading
ramp hummed through the entire frame of the massive helicopter.
By the time his crew chief could reach forward to slap an "all
secure" signal against his shoulder, they were already ten feet up
and fifty out. That was enough altitude. He kept the nose down
as he clawed for speed in the thin air at eleven thousand feet.

"Totally worth it," one of the D-boys announced as soon as
he was on the Chinook's internal intercom.

He'd have to remember to tell that to the two Black Hawks
flying guard for him…when they were in a friendly country
and could risk a radio transmission. This deep inside China—or
rather Chinese-held territory as the CIA's mission-briefing spook

had insisted on calling it—radios attracted attention and were only used to avoid imminent death and destruction.

"Great, now I just need to get us out of this alive."

"Do that, Pete. We'd appreciate it."

He wished to hell he had a stealth bird like the one that had gone into bin Laden's compound. But the one that had crashed during that raid had been blown up. Where there was one, there were always two, but the second had gone back into hiding as thoroughly as if it had never existed. He hadn't heard a word about it since.

The Tibetan terrain was amazing, even if all he could see of it was the monochromatic green of night vision. And blackness. The largest city in Tibet lay a mere ten kilometers away and they were flying over barren wilderness. He could crash out here and no one would know for decades unless some yak herder stumbled upon them. Or were yaks in Mongolia? He was a corn-fed, white boy from Colorado, what did he know about Tibet? Most of the countries he'd flown into on black ops missions he'd only seen at night anyway.

While moving very, very fast.

Like now.

The inside of his visor was painted with overlapping readouts. A pre-defined terrain map, the best that modern satellite imaging could build made the first layer. This wasn't some crappy, on-line, look-at-a-picture-of-your-house display. Someone had a pile of dung outside their goat pen? He could see it, tell you how high it was, and probably say if they were pygmy goats or full-size LaManchas by the size of their shit-pellets if he zoomed in.

On top of that were projected the forward-looking infrared camera images. The FLIR imaging gave him a real-time overlay, in case someone had put an addition onto their goat shed since the last satellite pass, or parked their tractor across his intended flight path.

His nervous system was paying autonomic attention to that combined landscape. He also compensated for the thin air at altitude as he instinctively chose when to start his climb over said goat shed or his swerve around it.

It was the third layer, the tactical display that had most of his attention. At least he and the two Black Hawks flying escort on him were finally on the move.

To insert this deep into Tibet, without passing over Bhutan or Nepal, they'd had to add wingtanks on the Black Hawks' hardpoints where he'd much rather have a couple banks of Hellfire missiles. Still, they had 20mm chain guns and the crew chiefs had miniguns which was some comfort.

While the action team was busy infiltrating the capital city and gathering intelligence on the particularly brutal Chinese assistant administrator, he and his crews had been squatting out in the wilderness under a camouflage net designed to make his helo look like just another god-forsaken Himalayan lump of granite.

Command had determined that it was better for the helos to wait on site through the day than risk flying out and back in. He and his crew had stood shifts on guard duty, but none of them had slept. They'd been flying together too long to have any new jokes, so they'd played a lot of cribbage. He'd long ago ruled no gambling on a mission, after a fistfight had broken out about a bluff hand that cost a Marine three hundred and forty-seven dollars. Marines hated losing to Army no matter how many times it happened. They'd had to sit on him for a long time before he calmed down.

Tonight's mission was part of an on-going campaign to discredit the Chinese "presence" in Tibet on the international stage—as if occupying the country the last sixty years didn't count toward ruling, whether invited or not. As usual, there was a crucial vote coming up at the U.N.—that, as usual, the Chinese could be guaranteed to ignore. However, the ever-hopeful CIA was in a hurry to make sure that any damaging information that they could validate was disseminated as thoroughly as possible prior to the vote.

Not his concern.

His concern was, were they going to pass over some Chinese sentry post at their top speed of a hundred and ninety-six miles an hour? The sentries would then call down a couple Shenyang J-16 jet fighters that could hustle along at Mach 2 to fry his sorry ass. He knew there was a pair of them parked at Lhasa along with some older gear that would be just as effective against his three helos.

"Don't suppose you could get a move on, Pete?"

"Eat shit, Nicolai!" He was a good man to have as a copilot. Pete knew he was holding on too tight, and Nicolai knew that a joke was the right way to ease the moment.

He, Nicolai, and the four pilots in the two Black Hawks had a long way to go tonight and he'd never make it if he stayed so tight on the controls that he could barely maneuver. Pete eased off and felt his fingers tingle with the rush of returning blood. They dove down into gorges and followed them as long as they dared. They hugged cliff walls at every opportunity to decrease their radar profile. And they climbed.

That was the true danger—they would be up near the helos' limits when they crossed over the backbone of the Himalayas in their rush for India. The air was so rarefied that they burned fuel at a prodigious rate. Their reserve didn't allow for any extended battles while crossing the border…not for any battle at all really.

# # #

It was pitch dark outside her helicopter when Captain Danielle Delacroix stamped on the left rudder pedal while giving the big Chinook right-directed control on the cyclic. It tipped her most of the way onto her side, but let her continue in a straight line. A Chinook's rotors were sixty feet across—front to back they overlapped to make the spread a hundred feet long. By cross-controlling her bird to tip it, she managed to execute a straight line between two mock pylons only thirty feet apart.

They were made of thin cloth so they wouldn't down the helo if you sliced one—she was the only trainee to not have cut one yet.

At her current angle of attack, she took up less than a half-rotor of width, just twenty-four feet. That left her nearly three feet to either side, sufficient as she was moving at under a hundred knots.

The training instructor sitting beside her in the copilot's seat didn't react as she swooped through the training course at Fort Campbell, Kentucky. Only child of a single mother, she was used to providing her own feedback loops, so she didn't expect anything else. Those who expected outside validation rarely survived the SOAR induction testing, never mind the two years of training that followed.

As a loner kid, Danielle had learned that self-motivated congratulations and fun were much easier to come by than external ones. She'd spent innumerable hours deep in her mind as a pre-teen superheroine. At twenty-nine she was well on her way to becoming a real life one, though Helo-girl had never been a character she'd thought of in her youth.

External validation or not, after two years of training with the U.S. Army's 160th Special Operations Aviation Regiment she was ready for some action. At least she was convinced that she was. But the trainers of Fort Campbell, Kentucky had not signed off on anyone in her trainee class yet. Nor had they given any hint of when they might.

She ducked ten tons of racing Chinook under a bridge and bounced into a near vertical climb to clear the power line on the far side. Like a ride on the toboggan at Terrassee Dufferin during *Le Carnaval de Québec,* only with five thousand horsepower at her fingertips. Using her Army signing bonus—the first money in her life that was truly hers—to attend *Le Carnaval* had been her one trip back after her birthplace since her mother took them to America when she was ten.

To even apply to SOAR required five years of prior military rotorcraft experience. She had applied after seven years because of a chance encounter—or rather what she'd thought was a chance encounter at the time.

Captain Justin Roberts had been a top Chinook pilot, the one who had convinced her to switch from her beloved Black Hawk and try out the massive twin-rotor craft. One flight and she'd been a goner, begging her commander until he gave in and let her cross over to the new platform. Justin had made the jump from the 10th Mountain Division to the 160th SOAR not long after that.

Then one night she'd been having pizza in Watertown, New York a couple miles off the 10th's base at Fort Drum.

"Danielle?" Justin had greeted her with the surprise of finding a good friend in an unexpected place. Danielle had liked Justin—even if he was a too-tall, too-handsome cowboy and completely knew it. But "good friend" was unusual for Danielle, with anyone, and Justin came close.

"Captain Roberts," as a dry greeting over the top edge of her Suzanne Brockmann novel didn't faze him in the slightest.

"Mind if I join ya?" A question he then answered for himself by sliding into the opposite seat and taking a slice of her pizza. She been thinking of taking the leftovers back to base, but that was now an idle thought.

"Are you enjoying life in SOAR?" she did her best to appear a normal, social human, a skill she'd learned by rote. *Greeting someone you knew after a time apart? Ask a question about them.* "They treating you well?"

"Whoo-ee, you have no idea, Danielle," his voice was smooth as…well, always…so she wouldn't think about it also sounding like a pickup line. He was beautiful, but didn't interest her; the outgoing ones never did.

"Tell me." *Men love to talk about themselves, so let them.*

And he did. But she'd soon forgotten about her novel, and would have forgotten the pizza if he hadn't reminded her to eat.

His stories shifted from intriguing to fascinating. There was a world out there that she'd been only peripherally aware of. The Night Stalkers of the 160th SOAR weren't simply better helicopter pilots, they were the most highly-trained and best-equipped ones on the planet. Their missions were pure razor's edge and black-op dark.

He'd left her with a hundred questions and enough interest to fill out an application to the 160th. Being a decent guy, Justin even paid for the pizza after eating half.

The speed at which she was rushed into testing told her that her meeting with Justin hadn't been by chance and that she owed him more than half a pizza next time they met. She'd asked after him a couple of times since she'd made it past the qualification exams—and the examiners' brutal interviews that had left her questioning her sanity, never mind her ability.

"Justin Roberts is presently deployed, ma'am," was the only response she'd ever gotten.

Now that she was through training—almost, had to be soon, didn't it?—Danielle realized that was probably less of an evasion and more likely to do with the brutal op tempo the Night Stalkers maintained. The SOAR 1st Battalion had just won the coveted Lt. General Ellis D. Parker awards for Outstanding Combat Aviation Battalion *and* Aviation Battalion of the Year. They'd been on deployment every single day of the last year, actually of the last decade-plus since 9/11.

The very first Special Forces boots on the ground in Afghanistan were delivered that October by the Night Stalkers and nothing had slacked off since. Justin might be in the 5th battalion D company, but they were just as heavily assigned as the 1st.

Part of their training had included tours in Afghanistan. But unlike their prior deployments, these were brief, intense, and then they'd be back in the States pushing to integrate their new skills.

SOAR needed her training to end and so did she.

Danielle was ready for the job, in her own, inestimable opinion. But she wasn't going to get there until the trainers signed off that she'd reached fully mission-qualified proficiency.

The Fort Campbell training course was never set up the same from one flight to the next, but it always had a time limit. The time would be short and they didn't tell you what it was. So she drove the Chinook for all it was worth like Regina Jaquess waterskiing her way to U.S. Ski Team Female Athlete of the Year.

The Night Stalkers were a damned secretive lot, and after two years of training, she understood why. With seven years flying for the 10th, she'd thought she was good.

She'd been repeatedly lauded as one of the top pilots at Fort Drum.

The Night Stalkers had offered an education in what it really meant to fly. In the two years of training, she'd flown more hours than in the seven years prior, despite two deployments to Iraq. And spent more time in the classroom than her life-to-date accumulated flight hours.

But she was ready now. It was *très viscérale,* right down in her bones she could feel it. The Chinook was as much a part of her nervous system as breathing.

Too bad they didn't build men they way they built the big Chinooks—especially the MH-47G which were built specifically to SOAR's requirements. The aircraft were steady, trustworthy, and the most immensely powerful helicopters deployed in the U.S. Army—what more could a girl ask for? But finding a superhero man to go with her superhero helicopter was just a fantasy for a lonely teenage girl.

She dove down into a canyon and slid to a hover mere inches over the reservoir inside the thirty-second window laid out on the flight plan.

Danielle resisted a sigh. She was ready for something to happen and to happen soon.

# # #

Pete's Chinook and his two escort Black Hawks crossed into the mountainous province of Sikkim, India ten feet over the glaciers and still moving fast. It was an hour before dawn, they'd made it out of China while it was still dark.

"Twenty minutes of fuel remaining," Nicolai said it like a personal challenge when they hit the border.

"Thanks, I never would have noticed."

It had been a nail-biting tradeoff: the more fuel he burned, the more easily he climbed due to the lighter load. The more he climbed, the faster he burned what little fuel remained.

Safe in Indian airspace he climbed hard as Nicolai counted down the minutes remaining, burning fuel even faster than he had been while crossing the mountains of southern Tibet. They caught up with the U.S. Air Force HC-130P Combat King refueling tanker with only ten minutes of fuel left.

"Ram that bitch," Nicolai called out.

Pete extended the refueling probe which reached only a few feet beyond the forward edge of the rotor blade and drove at the basket trailing behind the tanker on its long hose.

He nailed it on the first try despite the fluky winds. Striking the valve in the basket with over four hundred pounds of pressure, a clamp snapped over the refueling probe and Jet A fuel shot into his tanks.

His helo had the least fuel due to having the most men aboard, so he was first in line. His Number Two picked up the second refueling basket trailing off the other wing of the Combat King. Thirty seconds and three hundred gallons later and he was breathing much more easily.

"Ah," Nicolai sighed. "It is better than the sex," his thick Russian accent only ever surfaced in this moment or in a bar while picking up women.

"Hey, Nicolai," Nicky the Greek called over the intercom from his crew chief position seated behind Pete. "Do you make love in Russian?"

A question Pete had always been careful to avoid.

"For you, I make special exception." That got a laugh over the system.

Which explained why Pete always kept his mouth shut at this moment.

"The ladies, Nicolai? What about the ladies?" Alfie the portside gunner asked.

"Ah," he sighed happily as he signaled that the other choppers had finished their refueling and formed up to either side, "the ladies love the Russian. They don't need to know I grew up in Maryland and I learn my great-great-grandfather's native tongue at the University called Virginia."

He sounded so pleased that Pete wished he'd done the same rather than study Japanese and Mandarin.

Another two hours of—thank god—straight-and-level flight at altitude through the breaking dawn and they landed on the aircraft carrier awaiting them in the Bay of Bengal. India had agreed to turn a blind eye as long as the Americans never actually touched their soil.

Once standing on the deck—and the worst of the kinks worked out—he pulled his team together: six pilots and seven crew chiefs.

"Honor to serve!" He saluted them sharply.

"Hell yeah!" They shouted in response and saluted in turn. It was their version of spiking the football in the end zone.

A petty officer in a bright green vest appeared at his elbow, "Follow me please, sir." He pointed toward the Navy-gray command structure that towered above the carrier's deck. The Commodore of the entire carrier group was waiting for him just outside the entrance. Not a good idea to keep a One-Star waiting, so he waved at the team.

"See you in the mess for dinner," he shouted to the crew over the noise of an F-18 Hornet fighter jet trapping on the #2 wire. After two days of surviving on MREs while squatting on the Tibetan tundra, he was ready for a steak, a burger, a mountain of pasta, whatever. Or maybe all three.

The green escorted him across the hazards of the busy flight deck. Pete had kept his helmet on to buffer the noise, but even at that he winced as another Hornet fired up and was flung aloft by the catapult.

"Orders, Major Napier," the Commodore handed him a folded sheet the moment he arrived. "Hate to lose you."

The Commodore saluted, which Pete automatically returned before looking down at the sheet of paper in his hands. The man was gone before the import of Pete's orders slammed in.

A different green-clad deckhand showed up with Pete's duffle bag and began guiding him toward a loading C-2 Greyhound twin-prop airplane. It was parked number two for the launch catapult, close behind the raised jet-blast deflector.

His crew, being led across in the opposite direction to return to the berthing decks below, looked at him aghast.

"Stateside," was all he managed to gasp out as they passed.

A stream of foul cursing followed him from behind. Their crew was tight. Why the hell was Command breaking it up?

And what in the name of fuck-all had he done to deserve this?

He glanced at the orders again as he stumbled up the Greyhound's rear ramp and crash landed into a seat.

Training rookies?

It was worse than a demotion.

This was punishment.

Chapter 2

B*y the time the* C-130 transport jet he'd hitched a ride in across the country smacked down at Fort Campbell, Kentucky, Major Pete Napier still didn't know what to make of his orders. Command had clearly lost their marbles. And sending him out looking for them was just pissing him off.

But, when the orders had pulled him off of forward deployment and sent him stateside to test trainees, it had probably been a good career move *not* to call the Commodore who delivered the orders an ignorant ass. Navy Commodores didn't take any more kindly to such things than Army Brigadier Generals—no matter how richly the compliment might be deserved in both cases.

He hit the main desk at Fort Campbell with a severe dose of jet leg and a lethal dose of foul mood.

The desk orderly gave him a room key for the transient quarters in the Richardson Complex, informing him that it was for a maximum three-day occupancy so alternate arrangements should be made rapidly. As if base transient quarters were such a luxury. He managed not to execute the man on the spot, mostly because his sidearm was stowed in his duffle.

Pete didn't plan on being here longer than it took to track down his commander and talk his way back up to forward deployment. The trick was to do it without earning a court-martial for punching out a superior officer.

The guard also gave him a pass for the gate to the Night Stalkers compound and instructions to report immediately upon arrival to Colonel Cassius McDermott, the commander of the entire U.S. Army 160th Special Operations Aviation Regiment. Perfect. Exactly the man he needed to tackle.

Pete found a corporal to give him a lift, but was dumped unceremoniously outside the 160th's front gate with his gear. "Sorry, sir. I'm not authorized inside the compound."

The midday heat had baked into the pavement and was re-radiating with a vengeance as evening threatened to exceed a hundred-percent humidity even if it had to make up numbers to do it.

His body and his clothes were still oriented for the summer chill of Tibet and the not much warmer temperature of Air Force transports at altitude. He'd only been so much cargo to them: pressurized air was provided begrudgingly, heat not at all.

Pete thought wistfully of flying over the cool Himalayas as he slung on his pack and trudged through the heat, the blazing idiocy of security, and the long dusty stretch to the Colonel's on-base office—a bolthole for when he wasn't at the Pentagon doing whatever useless crap they performed there.

At least when Pete reported he was ushered straight into "the presence."

Colonel Cassius McDermott answered his salute with, "Pete, sit your sorry ass down. You look whipped, boy." He would have remained standing, but his legs didn't think that was really advisable at the moment and he collapsed into a chair.

"What the hell am I doing mingling with the recruits, Cass? And what's a One-Star doing messing with Night Stalker assignments?"

Cass McDermott had always been there for him: when Pete was a fresh-faced idiot Army National Guard pilot, when climbing the career ladder, even through an ugly marriage that led to an uglier divorce—all of it.

McDermott's field office was so plain that it might have belonged to a clerk, except for the photos of the Colonel shaking hands with each of the last three Presidents. The three photos and the American flag were the only relief to the colorlessness of the room; beige and khaki.

Cass leaned back in his chair and studied Pete through narrowed eyes like he was looking at a bug. Friend or not, the Colonel was like that. He wasn't just the commander of SOAR, he *was* SOAR. The man had flown every ugly mission there was for thirty years. But he didn't flaunt it. The only evidence of who this man really was appeared in the ever-expanding array of medals in the three progressive photos.

Rumor was they'd tried to promote him to JSOC half a dozen times and he'd refused. Well, Joint Special Operations Command's loss was definitely SOAR's gain. Pete respected few people beyond the cockpit, but McDermott was one of them.

"The Commodore was handy. They're actually my orders, but I figured I needed a bit of rank to deliver them so that you didn't spit in the messenger's face."

"Thought about doing more than spitting, but he'd already ducked and run."

"You don't rise to command an entire aircraft carrier group by being stupid."

Pete grimaced. He knew his reputation was bad, but *that bad?* He preferred being in the field, that was all. He didn't suffer fools lightly. That was a skill that a good trainer needed and he totally lacked.

McDermott looked at his watch and then back at Pete.

Pete had a sudden bad feeling about what was going to happen next, but the look on McDermott's face shifted as if he'd thought better of something.

"Tell you what. You go look the crew over and then we'll talk. I even provided you with a pair of ringers."

Pete waited, but the Colonel wasn't doing any explaining. Instead he rose to his feet, forcing Pete to struggle to his own.

"Here are the night's orders," McDermott handed over a single sheet of paper. He didn't give Pete time to look at them, instead offering a sharp salute. "I'll see you in eight hours. Dismissed."

Once in the outer office, Pete looked at the sheet. It would have been cryptography to anyone other than a Night Stalker.

To his trained eye, it read like only one thing.

He decided that Cass McDermott wasn't the only man who was wise enough to know when to duck. Cass had done it by making sure that Pete had been neatly ushered out of the Colonel's office before Pete had had a chance to look at the orders and heave them back in the Colonel's face.

He'd been awake for three days now and in ten minutes he was scheduled to face rookies.

Rookies!

Shit!

# # #

Captain Danielle Delacroix brushed a bang of dark hair out of her eyes and surveyed her classmates gathered in predictable clusters in front of the barracks that housed Special Operations Aviation Training Battalion. The hangar had been their semi-permanent home these last two years, when they weren't further afield training in the worst terrain the SOATB could find.

They had started with over a hundred and twenty men and six women. They now stood at eight and two, one of the highest graduation rates in history…if they'd graduated.

None of them were sure, and that was presently the sole topic of conversation, which frankly bored her to death at this point.

The 160th's trainers gave you information when you needed it and not a single second before. Second-guessing was a waste of effort, something she wasn't a big fan of.

Predictably, they were winging around a couple of Frisbees; so gob-smack frustrated that most of them had joined in rather than continue discussing their unknown future. They used glow-in-the-dark discs which, in the falling dusk, made their pale-green color almost impossible to see.

One whistled sharply when thrown due to a 7.62 millimeter hole some Al-Qaeda fanatic had shot through it. It belonged to the Might Quinn—a big Alaskan native. The Whistler was a real favorite among the crew, practically a mascot. It always sounded like a little cry to her when it flew. It was covered with signatures: some fresh and clear, others faded, some of the living, others who were no longer. Most of the trainees had signed it, perhaps all except her.

Stray throws came her way once or twice and she shot it back, but she remained separate, outside their game.

Their group still had a Sergeant and two Sergeants First Class who flew as crew chiefs and gunners in the back of the Chinook and Black Hawk helicopters.

The class had become small enough that a rotating group of instructor pilots were often sent to fill in the gaps—they needed two extra crew chiefs and one pilot whenever they all flew together.

Tonight's crew chiefs were a pair she'd never seen before: a big, powerful man who it was hard to imagine fitting in a helo, and a woman who barely came to his shoulder. They stood easily together off to the side with none of the foot-shifting and constant looking over their shoulders that marked the trainees.

The players winged a disc at them a couple of times as a test. Each time the big guy stretched out a long arm, snagged it out of the air, and then sent it pounding back so hard that a missed catch sent someone running a long way after it.

The pilots and copilots, if they were anywhere else, would have been divided by aircraft type: Little Birds, Black Hawks, and

Chinooks. But this was the U.S. Army's 160th Special Operations Aviation Regiment and the Night Stalkers were so far outside the curve that they tended to gather together regardless of the platform they flew. Or perhaps it was that if the pilots divided by platform they'd each be standing alone; there weren't many of them left after two years of training. Eighty-five percent hadn't made it out of the first three weeks.

A pair of Chief Warrants, one Second Lieutenant who had made the jump from being a backseater shortly before applying for SOAR, three Lieutenants, and herself—The Lone Captain. Didn't quite have the ring of *The Lone Ranger,* and she didn't even have a Tonto. As the sole remaining Chinook pilot, her copilot was always a trainer. And whoever he was, he was late.

It was odd how different the world was between those who flew in the backs of America's military helicopters and those who piloted the craft. She had tried to blend, but the line had been drawn deeply in prior service and even here few crossed between them—the Frisbee game making one of the few social bridges between the front and backseaters.

Danielle hadn't intended to turn "outsider" into a science any more than she'd meant to turn "gifted" into a reason to be isolated throughout her school years. She'd decided she had two choices, get angry every time they sat her close beside the teacher's desk so that she could be given advanced work that all of the other kids would resent, or become little Miss Perfect. Somewhere along about third grade, yet again the teacher's pet because she knew all of the answers, her brain discovered a third option.

She watched and she laughed, silently of course. People were about the funniest things on the planet. And, because she was such an outsider, no one ever dared ask what made her smile at the oddest of times. Danielle reached up a hand to check. Yes, she was smiling at the predictability of the groupings, right down to her own hermitic self.

To an outsider, there was very little to distinguish the candidates. It would appear that you could rearrange the pieces on this chessboard with no effect. All wore flightsuits and Army boots. They each had survival vests, FN-SCAR rifles strapped across their chests—though the ammunition was issued wrapped in plastic and you'd better have a damn good reason to have broken the security wrapper on U.S. soil—and helmets stacked off to the side of the game.

To an insider, it was only in knowing the individuals' habits and quirks that separated them, but that separation was obvious. Most of the crew chiefs had a free hand on one or another of their weapons when they weren't chasing the Frisbee. The pair of instructors also displayed this habit. Whereas pilots never knew what to do with their hands on the ground. They looked lost without a helicopter's cyclic and collective to hold onto, like a gamer looked when you suddenly unplugged his computer.

Other than the two new crew chiefs, she was the only one standing off to the side; disconnected, her hands in a studied neutral position. Originally she'd done it so that she could fit in with either group—and it worked for that. But she now understood that it also made her *not* fit in with either group.

Danielle had been called many things over her seven years in the U.S. Army before SOAR…actually for her entire life before applying to the 160th: aloof, distant, stuck up, men had called her lesbian, and lesbians had called her bitch.

She'd tried to leave that behind when she left the 10th Mountain Division to apply for SOAR, and mostly succeeded. Oh, she'd overheard conjectures that she didn't hit the town bars because she was a Mormon or had a lover back home who had made her promise never to enter a bar. In some tales her lover was male, other times a woman, and a few other typically Army suggestions involving both higher numbers and lower life forms that she chose to ignore.

She actually had no one waiting at home but by not commenting on the rumor of a hidden lover, it had grown and kept most of the unwanted attention away.

Danielle didn't go into bars because they were loud, smelly, and her mother was an alcoholic. She'd called Danielle close for what Danielle knew were her mother's last words—she'd asked for a gin and tonic. It used to make Danielle physically ill just to watch someone drink.

It was one of the things she liked about SOAR. They were on constant alert and the rules said twenty-four hours between a drink and a flight. Regular crews could count on a week off here and there, but not the trainees. There seemed to be a gleeful sadism among the trainers' cadre in promising vacation time and then blowing it up with a call-to-mission alert only after you were in transit.

Danielle had learned to work with the people of SOAR more smoothly because she completely owned the only currency that truly counted to the Night Stalkers—she flew better than almost anyone. It had been built into her DNA or blown into her bloodstream by a radioactive spider bite or something. She liked the idea of the spider. *Spidey rules!* If she ever met a man named Peter Parker she was going to marry him on the spot and they'd have superior radioactive children.

Danielle's secret identity wasn't her everyday self, it was her superhero occupation. When she was stuck in airports, restaurants, whenever out in public and the men came around—they always did—she'd use it. She learned quickly that she had to set the rules or they'd never go away.

Danielle invented the simplest of challenges to turn away the unwelcome attention.

"Guess what I do for a living. Three guesses and then you're gone. Guess right and I'll let you stay." Men understood bounded rules, even when the deck was stacked against them.

"Model."

"Actress."

"Singer/performer."

Those always took top spots. Especially country-western singer, which was odd since her bloodline and her accent were

Québécois French and her musical preferences were primarily medieval, through renaissance and baroque to the classical period. She danced to modern music—when absolutely no one was watching—but for listening Mozart was recent enough for her tastes.

No one had yet guessed military or even any kind of flying, other than—

"Stewardess."

—which she always corrected with…

"Flight attendant, but no."

Their general lack of creativity was astonishing. She eventually had tried announcing that she was none of the standard three right up front just to see what they came up with, but that stupefied most men into silence. Those who recovered invariably went to:

"Dental hygienist."

Someone had guessed:

"Language teacher."

Which she'd almost given him partial credit for. Like most Night Stalkers, she spoke several languages other than her native French and English. But then he'd followed up with:

"Porn star."

And she'd booted his ass.

Danielle belonged in the Night Stalkers, yet here she stood off to the side observing both herself and her classmates. She belonged but didn't. Which meant…

Her idle speculations were dragged beyond the gathering of trainees by the man stamping into view around the hangar from the direction of Regimental Command. Her missing Chinook copilot?

He moved like no Night Stalker she'd ever met, trainee or instructor. He moved with power and grace…and like a German Shepherd war dog ready to bite someone's head off.

# # #

Pete tramped past the rookies as if they weren't there, not even looking directly at them.

A few reacted, most didn't.

Someone sent a Frisbee winging by just feet in front of his nose. He considered pulling out his sidearm and shooting it out of the air. Instead he slapped it and left it where it rattled to a stop against the concrete pavement of the landing apron. The field was suddenly silent except for the distant roar of a C-130 taking off down the main Fort Campbell runway.

One of them, the one standing off to the side, had spotted him even as he rounded the hangar as if he'd been waiting for Pete's arrival.

Pete assessed the situation as he moved past them. One Black Hawk helicopter, squat and heavily armed with training rounds. One massive twin-rotor Chinook heavy-transport assault helo. Two Little Birds, both mission-enhanced as attack craft rather than for delivery or extraction. It was an odd mix, as were the puppy-panting hopefuls.

Pete continued to the Black Hawk, jerked open the massive side door. As it slid toward the rear of the helo, an oven-blast of trapped solar heat rolled over him. The remote Himalayas that he'd escaped just twenty-seven hours ago kept looking better and better.

While they waited or worried or whatever, he stripped down to his skivvies then dug out and donned his flightsuit that still reeked of too many hours spent squatting on the Tibetan soil with its foreign smells and dangerous feel. He grabbed his helmet and chucked the rest of the mess behind the rear cargo net.

When he turned back he noticed that the loner still watched him. Cool behind dark shades despite the failing light, narrow face, well-defined features…and dark brunette hair down to his shoulders.

Shit!

Her shoulders.

And it fell in one of those slightly disarrayed cascades women never understood was a hundred times sexier than the fanciest hairdo. Or maybe they did.

He scanned the others. The redhead, also clearly female, also watched him closely, though she had a wide and saucy grin. He must be even more exhausted than he'd thought, to miss them.

Women. Two.

He knew the 160th's 5th Battalion D Company had women, both crew chiefs and pilots, and he wouldn't wish that hell on anyone. He'd lost good fliers, ones he thought were good men, to rape charges because they couldn't keep their dick in their pants, fraternization courts-martial, or simply falling in goddamn love and losing their edge as they worried more about "home and family" than the person trying to shoot them out of the sky. Good men turned into "lovesick bull calves" like whatever that old movie was.

Now he was probably going to get his ass hauled in by one of them because he'd changed clothes right out in the open. Well, to hell with them. And he'd kept his underwear on, hadn't he? He was too tired to be sure. Or to care.

Thank god this assignment was only temporary.

"You! Specialty?" he snapped out as he moved over to the loner. There was always one in every group.

"Civility, sir," she answered with a light French accent and a deadpan tone that almost made him smile. That was pretty unexpected given his current frame of mind. But it wasn't your average soldier who could tell a superior officer he was being an ass so graciously.

"Civil Sybil? Woman of many personalities?"

# # #

Danielle could feel the cusp before her. She'd earned a hundred "tags" over the last nine years, but none had stuck, though they sometime took months to shed. She could feel "Sybil" hovering in the air, but she had no interest in being tagged with a nickname implying multiple personality disorder. Very *not* superhero.

Specialty? She'd flown in all three birds. The Little Bird as a copilot just so she could viscerally know what they could do. She liked the tactile knowledge, had ultimately run it through the obstacle course without killing herself or her pilot. She was technically still qualified to Readiness Level 1 on the Black Hawk, but not to SOAR standards. She done the yearly requisite basics to still be qualified to fly one around—more out of stubbornness than need—but she'd never be dumb enough to take one into battle.

Her training and reflexes had been honed to a single craft.

She pointed at the big Chinook. That was the monster helicopter of the Army, and SOAR's MH-47Gs were equipped like no others in the entire American fleet. Much to her own surprise, SOAR had taught her that the big beast was more than her favorite craft, it was her baby.

The man eyed her skeptically. He wore no rank, had offered no salute. He looked haggard and frustrated and she considered offering him a moment of sympathy. Then his piercing brown eyes focused on her.

"What was the hesitation?"

"Sybil aside," she did her best to drive that tag off the map, "I have a specialty, I am Basic Mission Qualified in the Chinook. But I am also still rated RL1 and served as a pilot-in-command in the Black Hawk with the 10th Mountain. I also have thirty hours in the Little Bird in which I'd rank myself as a Readiness Level 3 at best." RL3 was flight school-level skilled, nothing practical for the real world.

He squinted at her in disbelief; she couldn't tell if it was of the mock or macho-chauvinist variety. It felt as if she was back at the three questions stage of fending off unwanted men.

"Nobody flies all three. Hell, I don't fly all three."

She held up three fingers for emphasis and resisted the urge to lower all but the middle one. Granted it was pretty damn unusual—pilots spent their entire career in just one platform—but she was as she'd said, and to hell with him whoever he was.

"Wait, you said you were Basic Mission Qualified?"

"We all were. Eighteen months ago."

The guy slapped at his pockets looking for something. She finally pointed at the sheet of paper clutched in his hand.

He sighed then read it carefully.

"Not rookies."

"We've all had two years of every hell the Instructor Pilots could put us through and six one-month tours overseas."

"One-month tours? That's whacked." He shook his head, like a wet dog trying to clear his ears.

How was she supposed to judge what was whacked and what was normal for SOAR?

"Three platforms, huh?" he eyed her more carefully, head to foot and back. "Cerberus perhaps?"

She had to duck her head for a moment to not laugh in his face. Probably not a good move if he was her training pilot for the night. And image of the guy as the three-headed puppy dog guarding the gates of Hell felt totally appropriate; especially for calling her the Hell Hound.

"This is not the Three Dog Night. I prefer the three sister-Fates." Danielle lowered her tone and added some volume, "Beware mortal for I am Atropos and I shall sever thy thread ere it is fully spun."

"Caution, for I am Clotho," he replied without so much as an eyeblink. "Without me there is no spun thread for you to cut nor your sister to measure." He moved off toward the others without further comment.

She'd had strange discussions before with different commanders. Never had she spouted Ancient Greek myths at one, and he didn't look like the sort to reply in kind as easily as most guys did with football scores. Danielle followed in his wake.

"Who else here has flown in all three platforms?"

No one responded.

"Two?"

Rafe's hand went up—at least some familiarity was a standard part of SOAR training and Rafe had done well enough in the Little Bird—but the taciturn commander could read the tentativeness as clearly as Danielle could. Had he asked "Basic Mission Qualified in two platforms" Rafe's hand would still be down as would hers.

The two new crew chiefs also raised their hands—with decidedly more confidence than Rafe's—which was almost more unusual than a pilot who had flown all three.

"Well, you know your birds, go to them."

Rafe and Julian headed for the Black Hawk.

The Mighty Quinn and M&M headed for the two Little Birds.

The man looked at her, "You called it, Atropos. Get thee to thy Chinook."

She heard the Shakespearean line of Hamlet to his Ophelia of "Get thee to a nunnery"—a nunnery in Elizabethan times being a whorehouse.

"With the God Zeus *himself* as my copilot?" She wanted to stuff his arrogance back down his throat.

The smile didn't touch his lips, but it might have lurked briefly near his eyes. "What misbegotten idea makes you think that I'm not the pilot in command?"

"Because, despite what the others think, my sixth sense says that our training is not yet complete."

"You and Spiderman?"

"Spiderwoman." Spiderman had rocking superpowers; there had already been a Supergirl and a Catwoman, it was about time for a new heroine. She offered him a curt nod and her best smile before heading over to the Chinook.

# # #

Pete watched the slight woman head for the massive helicopter. Even the bulk of the flightsuit couldn't beef her up. She stood several inches shorter than his six feet. Call it five-eight. Her boot size was small and her hands had looked fine and delicate as she held up the three fingers. But he'd also been able to easily see the one-finger salute she'd been considering. He liked spunk, especially when he was being an asshole and deserved it. She also had an education, though it remained to be seen if she had brains to go with it.

Then she had dug up that laser bright smile. He'd figured her as over-educated and dour. Getting a smile for a comic book reference was the last thing he'd expected. And one that shifted her face from merely beautiful to…

He sure as hell wasn't going to follow that thought no matter how exhausted he was.

Pete let the crew chiefs sort themselves out. McDermott's two "ringers" were easy to spot even if they hadn't raised their hands. Since they both claimed multiple platforms, he sent the big guy to the Chinook and the other—crap, another woman—to keep an eye on the rookies aboard the Black Hawk. He wanted to assess the group's strengths and weaknesses.

SOAR crews flew out at the edge. Special Operations depended on them for extreme results, whether flying undetected into the heart of Tibet or racing the Pakistani jets after landing in bin Laden's compound. The isolation of training was about to be broken for these folks.

"Move it out," he ordered.

"Yes sir, oh mighty laird of the clans," the redhead offered in a bright Irish brogue that rang distinctly of one of those New England cities.

He let it go, let them get a head start, then strolled among the aircraft as they went over them. There wouldn't be anything to find, SOAR had the best mechanics in the business, but no crew flew an aircraft they hadn't preflighted themselves no matter a ground mechanic's signature on an airworthiness certificate.

They soon had their flashlights out as the sunset had finished turning blue sky into red. The occasional transport jet flashed into the sky along one of the runways, but otherwise the area was quiet. Only the Night Stalkers were based on this side of Fort Campbell.

Without asking names, he began mentally tagging them.

He'd be joining Spiderwoman, two of the crew chiefs, and the big guy ringer on the MH-47G Chinook.

The pair of pilots in the Black Hawk could have been twins if one wasn't six inches taller and the other one black. He considered "Pete" and "Repete" but didn't want the confusion with his own name, so he went with "3PO" and "R2." Another crew chief and the female ringer landed there.

That left two MH-6M Little Birds with a pilot and copilot each.

One of the Little Bird pilots practically vibrated with energy, a good match for the fast and agile craft. "Bunny." The copilot attracted no name in particular, a tall gawky nerd. Pete tagged him with "Geek" for now.

The second Little Bird pilot was the one he'd expected to head for the heavy Chinook; Pete dubbed him "Dozer" for his powerful build. The redheaded woman was his copilot.

"Got a name, Mister?" she asked when she spotted him watching her preflight her helo.

"I do, Boston."

"I'm from Gloucester."

"Right," he moved on, leaving "Boston" cursing his back. At least she had the good sense from her years in the service to do so silently.

When he reached the Chinook, the feel was different. The two trainee crew chiefs were moving sharp and silent over the craft chasing after the circles of light cast by their flashlights. The ringer showed all the signs of extreme competence, but it wasn't the big guy the trainees were reacting to. The crew chiefs moved as if in fear of something.

He couldn't put his finger on it until the loner brunette pilot circled around the nose of the craft. She wasn't up in her cockpit; she was doing her own walk-around, a habit that he wholly approved of. The crew chiefs were afraid of…her? No. Of not being up to her standard? Actually, yeah. He could see by the way she was inspecting the craft that she missed nothing and every man-jack of her crew knew it.

Unexpected in a newly trained SOAR pilot; he liked it. Despite his preferences for male-only combat crews, he liked her.

The Chinook MH-47G was a monster. It could lift fifteen tons of gear or a platoon of troops and deliver it fifteen thousand feet up. The rear cargo ramp was wide enough for a Humvee to load aboard and the main bay could hold two of them at once. It flew with two pilots and three crew chiefs who manned the cargo bay gun positions.

The helicopter should have dwarfed this woman, but instead it made her seem larger.

Pete moved up into the cockpit and settled into the copilot's seat, for she had been absolutely right. The training might be done, but the final test wasn't.

That was tonight's mission. Find their limits and then push past them.

Chapter 3

By the time the aircraft were all spun up and ready to go, the sunset had wound down and the four helos were nothing but green, white, and red running lights on the concrete apron in front of the Fort Campbell hangars.

"Everyone sleep well today?" Pete wished he had, but he'd never been one for snoozing off on a transport plane. Even with earplugs they were too bloody loud. Of course, he'd taken two hundred and fifty bucks off the other grunts stuck aboard the flight in a quick round of poker, so he wasn't complaining. He didn't release the mike switch for them to answer.

"We have a flight tonight. If your altitude crosses above two hundred feet, you will automatically fail and be returned to your unit." Not true, but it didn't hurt to scare them a bit. "If you cross over one-fifty you will want to pass every other aspect of this test *perfectly*—none of the criteria for that will be explained beforehand."

He could feel the indrawn breath around him. *That's right, people. Graduation exam time.* That's what had been on the orders from Colonel McDermott; though he'd still have to corner Cass as to why he'd dragged Pete half-around the planet to run the test.

"The planned flight level for this test is fifty feet. The Chinook is taller and gets an allowance to sixty feet."

He paused, expected a huff of complaint from the woman beside him. The Chinook wasn't merely ten feet taller. It was also long, wide, and heavy. That much craft needed space to maneuver and he wasn't giving it to her.

But she sat immobile behind her helmet's closed visor, left hand resting on the collective beside her seat and the right on the cyclic between her knees as if she was a machine merely ready to be turned on.

And there was a dumb image. He was *not* turned on by beautiful women who flew massive helicopters. It simply wouldn't do.

…as if she was a machine ready to start.

"Anyone who wanders more than three rotor diameters from the Chinook, do us all a favor and simply quit now." The Chinook's rotor was sixty feet across; the front and rear rotors overlapping for a total diameter of a hundred feet. He'd give them that much. Three hundred feet sounded like a lot, until you were following the terrain at a hundred and fifty miles an hour in a ten-ton chunk of steel.

Pete knew that when all combined, these were stricter requirements than any mission they'd flown in the last two years—stricter than what was in the orders as well, but they didn't need to know that. It had been five years and he could still feel the fear in his gut from that last day of training, not that he'd showed it any more than the woman sitting next to him was. See how she was doing by the end of the flight.

"First stop is," he read off a set of coordinates quickly and by his tone made it clear he wouldn't be repeating them. "Little Birds will have seven minutes to refuel." The Little Birds could travel only half the distance of their two big brothers. They were short strike craft that were going to be pushing their limits tonight.

The Sister-Fate Spiderman—Spiderwoman, crap!—had punched the coordinates into the navigation console as he read them. He stared at the terrain map she pulled up and managed not to laugh.

"Which is a swamp in central Mississippi." It was not going to be a pleasant refueling site. The Little Birds would have to hover in place for the entire seven minutes, shifting their controls to compensate for the growing fuel load as their tanks were refilled. And do it without ticking off or killing the waiting ground crew.

"Now, move it!"

He had to give them credit. If anyone hesitated, he couldn't see it.

# # #

Danielle had seen his type before. Arrogant and, only through the courtesy of modern military command training, not quite displaying what an asshole he was. Clearly the Equal Opportunity training of Army Regulation 600-20 and Command Training Guidance course on Sensitivity had been even more of a burden on him than it had on her.

For her, she'd been pissed at having to take all the classes that certified her as being human and having rights. As a trained and armed Special Operations Forces soldier she could damn well enforce her own rights.

For him…that's why they'd written the *imbécile* courses in the first place. The attempt to evolve him from Neanderthal to Early Cro-Magnon had clearly been a gamble that had only marginally paid off. That he was a nice-looking asshole with a quirky sense of humor and the education to use it well didn't change the base noun despite the assorted adjectives.

He hadn't even set the intercom to automatically include the crew. She preferred to run an open channel throughout the craft, but *Monsieur Imbécile* hadn't set it that way when he was done with the radio. No, it wasn't his doing. It already had been set to isolate the cockpit and she hadn't changed that during preflight. And since he wasn't helping her, she couldn't free up a hand to change the setting.

She crossed the two-lane security road of Nightstalker Way, edged over the Fort Campbell back fence, and rolled up the hills to the tree line. She chose a path that kept her rotors above the trees but slalomed her aircraft's body down among the treetops. Special ten-foot dispensation for her Chinook? To hell with that.

He did nothing to assist her flight, which made the Chinook a huge challenge. It was a complex craft that required two experienced pilots, especially if she was planning to survive a long distance Nap of Earth flight. NOEs required perfect concentration and fast reflexes…and on a Chinook MH-47G moving at a hundred-and-fifty knots, *it required two goddamn people.*

"Did you say something?" His Imperial Namelessness asked over the intercom.

"Not a word," at least she didn't think she had. But now that he mentioned it, "How about you start doing your goddamn copilot's job, sir?" She led the flight of four helos west until she picked up Kentucky Lake. Ten feet above the water she turned south and crossed into Tennessee.

"All you had to do was ask," suddenly he was all *le chevalier* Sir Sweetness-and-Light. In moments he'd cleaned up a half-dozen settings, adjusted the throttle sync on the two Honeywell T55 turboshaft engines so that the irritating beat frequency of their slightly different speeds became far less annoying, and rested his hands on the controls as a backup to her own motions.

"Damned lucky I need both hands to fly this thing," she muttered to herself.

"Or you'd be snipping my thread?" he returned jovially.

She really needed to learn to keep her mutters to herself. Or first make sure that no one was there to hear. "I thought I was Spiderwoman. If that was truth, you'd be lucky that I need both hands to fly or I'd plaster your face with the stickiest web I could come up with."

"She both spins threads and cuts them. Half Spidey and half Atropos. You got a name, pilot?"

"Only if you do."

He laughed.

Who knew the taciturn bastard could laugh. It was a good laugh and she liked it despite being fairly convinced that she hated him thoroughly.

"Pete."

"Not Peter?"

"Not even on my birth certificate. Parents named me Pete."

"That's a relief."

"Why?"

"Because if your name was Peter Parker then—" she cut herself off before she could sound even more stupid about how she'd have to marry him.

"Major Pete Napier at your service."

Danielle almost bobbled the controls at that. She'd been teasing Pete "The Rapier" Napier? He was notorious throughout the five battalions of SOAR and beyond, right into her former Falcons—10th Mountain Division, Combat Aviation Brigade, 3rd Battalion, 10th Regiment. She'd worked to get assigned to the 10th of the 10th because they flew the same three birds as the Night Stalkers, less advanced versions but still it had let her learn what all three types were truly capable of.

But The Rapier?

"Captain Danielle Delacroix at your service, Major," she managed to keep her voice neutral.

She'd studied his techniques almost as much as those of the legendary Majors Beale and Henderson. Major Napier was one of the top pilots in all SOAR. He sent back techniques to be added into training that were nearly irreproducible...and he'd come up with them while flying combat which made them downright miraculous.

Unlike Beale and Henderson, who were *famous* within the SOAR community, *notorious* was the proper adjective for Major Napier. Notorious for being a total hard ass. No one flew farther out on the edge than Pete Napier.

He was also the reason she'd ultimately given in to Justin Roberts' attempts to get her to switch to the Chinook; Major Napier was generally acknowledged as the master of the MH-47 throughout SOAR. *Keep it light, Danielle. Keep it light.*

"Napier?" she managed to say his name as if maybe it was French or, if not, perhaps it should be. Though if she'd been a teenaged boy, her voice would have cracked horridly in a total fan-girl moment.

Kentucky Lake had led to the Tennessee River. She rode through the sharp oxbow bend at Waverly and watched how the others were keeping formation on her. Rafe's Black Hawk held tight as did Quinn's Little Bird. "Tighten up, M&M." The second Little Bird pulled in closer until they were a flying wedge of death.

"M&M? I thought of him as Energizer, like the bunny because of how he moves."

"Lieutenant Manfred Malcolm. M&M."

"He'll be in trouble if he ever makes my rank," Major Napier's voice remained deadpan.

"Napier?" mangling it with a Italian accent this time. "Jack or the butler?" Let's see if he was half as sharp as he thought he was. Jack Napier had been The Joker's name in the Michael Keaton *Batman* movie. Alan Napier had been the actor who played Alfred the Butler in the original TV series.

"Oh, I dare say, madam," Pete made his voice butler-pompous, but no Michael Caine-English accent which would have been inappropriate for Alan Napier. "I am not cruel."

Unlike his reputation.

Well, The Rapier wasn't known for cruelty, not exactly. It was more a combination of vicious and lethal. His battle-plan attacks consistently struck at the very core of the enemy with an overwhelming force, even when the core was deceptively hidden. He had a strategic sense that made his attacks master strokes that the enemy could not evade.

Danielle kept low to the water, made sure everyone was well inside the training envelope of three rotor diameters. But mostly she watched the terrain map inside her visor for stray bridges and water-crossing power lines…and potential enemy surprises. This was a training flight, perhaps their final one, and there were bound to be at least one or two engagements to test their mettle.

Napier yawned loudly into the intercom and she remembered the exhausted look as he'd arrived from Command.

"When was the last time you slept, sir?"

"Before Tibet. Shit! I did not just say that," he scrabbled at the communication system and then huffed out a sigh of relief when his finger tapped against the switch set to isolate the cockpit's intercom. "You, Captain, are not authorized for that information. Are we clear?"

"I can only assume you were hunting for a blue flower at the base of a mountain topped by a league of evil assassins." And now that she'd evoked the image, she wished she hadn't. Christian Bale had been seriously hot in *Batman Begins*. And only now did it register quite how much Napier looked like Bale. She'd certainly gotten an eyeful when he'd stripped down to change into his flightsuit back at Fort Campbell. Bale had worked out for the role, whereas Pete the Rapier had done soldiering for a career and the difference showed. He was remarkably fit; that was a safe word for a commanding officer wasn't it? Very remarkably—

Keep your mind on your flying, girl!

Knowing he had his hands on the controls, she released the collective for a moment and set the intercom to the whole aircraft. The sounds inside her helmet expanded to include the crew chatting quietly on the other circuit, making sure they were staying sharp. It also served to inform Pete the Rapier that she wouldn't be pursuing his unintended comment.

Didn't mean she couldn't think about it though.

Tibet, huh? A politically impossible mission, because even a whiff of American military on Chinese soil would have created a major international incident. Things certainly weren't going to be dull once she'd passed into the Night Stalkers. If this was the graduation exercise, it meant that her real missions were about to begin. Finally!

While it was easy to file away thoughts of Tibet, the image of flying with Pete the Rapier dressed only in his briefs as her personal butler wasn't going to go away anytime soon.

# # #

Pete kept an eye on the pair of Little Birds as they were refueling in a swamp along the Black Warrior River watershed of northern Alabama.

The ground team would report on just how well they did, but they looked good from where he sat forty feet up and a hundred yards to the side in the Chinook. SOAR training had made sure these people were good or they would have long since been washed out.

But were they good enough?

The attack came a quarter mile after they left the refuel point. He knew it was inevitable even if he didn't know when.

The trainees hadn't a clue.

Two AH-64 Apache gunships waited side by side around a bend in the river. At the far edge of the tactical display he also spotted an F/A-18E Super Hornet jet coming down from fifty thousand feet, at least it wasn't moving at supersonic speeds. Still, a nasty scenario. Personally, he might have added another helo coming from behind.

Danielle burped the radio, "Craft please identify."

What came back from the Apaches in response were a pair of missiles, at least simulated ones.

"Flares and up," she called on the encrypted frequency.

"Up" was not a choice he would have made, especially with the jet descending from above. Clearly she hadn't spotted the jet out at the very edge of the display.

Of course with "Down" they were under twenty feet from hitting the soggy soil. Most students went to the sides which exposed their bellies to the Apache attackers and also counted as a kill.

All four choppers rolled upward. As they hit vertical they all triggered their flares. Bright flares shot out to the sides of each helicopter which would hopefully distract a heat-seeking missile. The helos climbed in such a tight formation that the flares created a veritable wall of shining light between their four helos and the attacking Apaches.

For the moment, the Apaches' night-vision gear would be overwhelmed.

As Danielle pulled vertical she called, "Jules, two away on the jet."

So she had seen it.

The Black Hawk unleashed a pair of simulated Hellfire missiles and sent them streaking directly up at the diving F/A-18E Super Hornet. The fake missiles fizzled after a hundred yards and would fall harmlessly to the swamp where a follow-up team would recover them. But the jet's computers decided it was dead and out of the game.

"Mighty and M&M," was her next call, with no additional instructions and Pete could only wait to see what they came up with.

The Chinook and the Black Hawk continued their loops, but rolling over sideways as they did so. Instead of flying onto their backs, they were once again upright and diving back down to the riverbed the way they'd come.

The two Little Birds had done the opposite. Hidden behind the wall of flares, they'd climbed and then nosed over until they were diving on the Apaches from above. They burst clear of the bright wall painted by the flares, firing simulated chain guns.

The Apaches' sensors registered that they were destroyed just moments later.

"Maximum height during engagement?" Danielle called out.

"Shit!" one of the Little Bird pilots swore.

Pete double checked the readouts. He'd told them that the plan was fifty, they'd be on probation over one hundred and fifty feet and would fail over two hundred feet. A total lie. After two years of training, SOAR didn't discard pilots that lightly, but he wanted to see what they could do.

The swearing Little Bird pilot had hit a hundred and thirty feet as he nosed over. The other bird hadn't even crossed a hundred. Clearly Danielle had held them to a higher standard.

"Re-form. Continue mission," Pete snapped out trying his best to sound irritated.

In silence they formed up around her once more and continue to roar south along the Black Warrior River.

"Mighty?" he asked over the Chinook's intercom to avoid complimenting Danielle on the exceptional maneuver. Plus he wanted to prompt her into speaking more. He generally appreciated a closed-mouth pilot, but that French accent of hers was about the only thing keeping him sharp…he could listen to it all day.

"The big Alaskan guy, Mickey Quinn. We call him The Mighty Quinn from the Bob Dylan song *Quinn the Eskimo*."

"I thought of him as Dozer."

"The Mighty Dozer? Bet he'd like that."

Pete didn't want to be as impressed as hell, especially not by a bunch of trainees, but he was anyway. He'd flown with new teams before and they didn't function the way this one had. Hell, he'd flown with fully qualified teams that couldn't do that last maneuver…or would think to.

There was the difference to this group and he'd bet that he knew its source.

# # #

"All craft."

Danielle had already learned enough about The Rapier's tone of voice to know that bad news was incoming.

"During the last engagement, Captain Danielle Delacroix was critically injured. I am a Chief Warrant Two only RL2 on the Chinook platform."

Which meant he could fly well enough, but don't depend on him to complete the mission.

"The mission is critical, continue on profile. Out."

"I'm not—"

"I need to see how much they rely on you, Delacroix, because I'm betting that whole last piece was you're doing."

"But they need to know I'm not—"

"Shut up, Spidey."

A bark of laughter over the Chinook's internal intercom told her that she'd better like that tag because she'd just become stuck with it—at least for a while. Maybe a long while.

She wanted to argue, but it was true. The jet had been unexpected, but by chance she'd penciled out everything else about this exact scenario a few months ago and they'd made it a mental puzzle over dinner. That it had come off so seamlessly made her damn proud of the team, and more than a little surprised at herself. She hadn't really expected it to work so neatly in the real world.

Rafe "Yank" Grant, the Black Hawk's pilot, took command. He'd been tagged the day he told how his slave ancestors had chosen their last name after Ulysses S. Grant had freed the South—despite his thick Georgia accent. Yank shifted the Chinook back into the pocket with himself in the lead and a Little Bird to either side.

"Is 'Yank' the tall white one or the little black guy?" Napier asked her.

"The little one," she replied. Yank was shorter than she was, but she'd never thought of him as little. He was solidly broad-shouldered, serious, and an exceptional pilot. They were constantly pushing at each other. "Kenny flies copilot."

When Rafe asked for Pete's name—she was still the only one who knew who was flying with them—Napier simply replied, "Call me Butler."

Unintentionally, her snort of laughter went out over the air. She could feel the others relax, see it in how they flew. And if "The Butler" didn't like that she'd just revealed she was uninjured, screw him.

"Did you consider having your Black Hawk drive straight ahead through the flare wall?" Pete asked her as if they were all hers to order and command. Yank led them once more along the Black Warrior River and passed the "dead" Apaches who rocked side to side in a wave before turning for home.

She hadn't. "That seems a desperate maneuver. The Black Hawk would take severe damage."

"Think about it. There are times when enemy air traffic radar is only a hundred feet over your head and you couldn't have done your little climb."

She'd never contemplated sacrificing one of her crew. Of course, the 10th Mountain Division wasn't about being subtle, it was about being so obviously overwhelming that the enemy turned tail and ran or was destroyed in place. The 10th Mountain was likely to throw twenty or more helos at a battle—backed up by a dozen M1 Abrams tanks along with other odds and ends—to humble the enemy into submission.

SOAR was all about subtle and would send two or three. The seven, or perhaps eight, that they sent against bin Laden had been a massive campaign by Night Stalker standards.

She continued to do the flying and Pete The Rapier continued to bring it down on their heads. But with each engagement he would ask her one or two questions that would force her to completely rethink the scenario. He was so good, and so far inside her head, that he knew exactly what she'd missed.

It wasn't just a one-way flow of information though. His voice was always sharper when the crew did something he hadn't expected. He dug after every nuance of her thinking about those situations, and always followed her last answer with a, "Huh."

At first she thought she was being accused of screwing up. Then she understood that he wasn't being aggressive, he was learning. From her and the team. He pursued each morsel of knowledge as if it truly mattered. The other trainees had appreciated—eventually—the results of her obsessive "beating the facts to death."

Pete was the first pilot who she couldn't leave behind in that mental pursuit. He was right there with her and it was… completely the wrong thought…sexual in its power—the back and forth as they both strove to be better.

Eight hours, five Little Bird refuelings, two mid-air refuels for the Chinook and the Black Hawk, and seven attacks later, everyone was still alive…except for her, of course. They'd recovered a team of SEALs out on the Gulf of Mexico and redeployed them in a staged attack against a "terrorist held" oil platform. And still she was "dead." But even the attacks they hadn't discussed previously as possible scenarios had gone off smoothly enough using tactics she'd helped create.

Danielle might not know what to do with people on the ground, but god she totally rocked it in the air, even when she wasn't the one giving the instructions.

# # #

They settled to ground in a remote corner of Fort Rucker Army Airfield an hour before sunrise. It was the absolute center of all Army heli-aviation training.

The four helicopters of their flight clustered at the far end of the otherwise empty Ech Army Stagefield Heliport.

Pete stripped off his helmet and went blind. All of the information that had been feeding into his visor—flight data, engine status, tactical overlay, night-vision territorial view—was gone and now he was sitting in the dark.

He slumped in the seat and closed his eyes. Two days in Tibet, a day in transit, and an eight-hour graduation test flight. The exhaustion was past palpable and actually made him nauseous.

"Someone has it in for me."

"Who might that be?" Danielle asked in that lovely French ripple of hers. He could hear her finishing the shutdown checklists. He should be helping but he was too damn tired.

"My money is on Colonel Cassius McDermott. Oh crap. You—"

"—didn't hear that, I know. You must be more careful, *Monsieur* Rapier, so that you are not snipping your own thread."

He stared out the broad windscreen of the Chinook at the blacked-out heliport, with only vague outlines of trees and a few stars showing. He'd been to Mother Rucker, as everyone called the Fort, innumerable times—for all Army pilots returned to the Mother throughout their career for everything from periodic tests with instructor pilots to advanced training. And the trainers were total motherfuckers in how hard they drove you, so it all fit.

The Fort had a dozen of these stagefields scattered about the local counties for training, but Pete had never used Ech. By the look of it, no one else had in a long time. He'd barely heard of it. In all his flights around the area, he couldn't be sure he'd even passed over this field. Were all flights routed around it? There was an interesting thought.

Hanchey, Knox, Lowe, and Shell heliports all had a hundred or more tie-down spots for individual helos. Only the main airfield at Cairns had runways for fixed-wing aircraft. They all had lights and instrument approaches. The big Stagefields like Allen, Brown, and Runkie did as well. Not Ech.

Ech had nine tie-downs, five short runways appropriate for practicing rolling and emergency landings. There was one small building that had definitely seen better days and was barely big enough for a half dozen offices. Close beside it was a hangar that looked brand new—at least it had through the night-vision gear as they'd descended—and was big enough for a half dozen birds.

The heliport was surrounded by a curtain of trees and was three miles of narrow dirt road from the next nearest piece of Mother Rucker.

He looked out into the darkness but they were the only ones there. This was the last set of coordinates on the training document, so it was the right place. But it certainly didn't say what to do next.

Shit!

That's what he'd landed in, a total shithole. Right down the old crapper.

Spiderwoman clicked on a cabin light and pulled off her own helmet. He blinked at the surprising brightness, and then again at Captain Danielle Delacroix. He hadn't been this close to her without her helmet on. Or if he had, he'd been blind. Her features weren't merely fine, they were elegant. And when she dug her fingers through her hair, the helmet hair went away and the thick mane of dark brown flowed once more down to her shoulders.

He'd noticed her beauty before, he must have, but he'd seen her as a female burr upon his own existence. However, burrs upon his existence didn't fly as well as she had. And about to be graduated trainees never ever functioned so cleanly as a team.

"You are staring, Monsieur Butler."

Pete was. And he wasn't having much luck stopping. That French accent of hers only added to the fine picture she painted. Let Spidey keep Kirsten Dunst, this was his idea of beauty.

She snapped her fingers right in front of his face and forced him to blink.

"Sorry," he rubbed at his face and it made no difference. "It's been three or four days since I slept and you're gorgeous. And I can't believe I just said that either." He couldn't read the reaction on her face. There was one, but he couldn't read it.

"No more than you said the other thing which I have already forgotten. I truly think you should sleep more often, Major Napier."

Just that simply she targeted and destroyed the easy mood that had settled over them during the flight. The teasing tone hadn't particularly shifted, but the message had totally changed. His rank and name now stood between them, as did six years of flying for the Night Stalkers.

By the time they had the helos shut down, log books completed, and the crews had exited their birds, the first light of day was ghosting to life somewhere over the horizon toward Georgia.

They were the last ones to exit down the long length of the Chinook's cargo hold, only the slightly pale square of the open cargo ramp guiding them forward. The heat was already oppressive and right in front of him, Danielle began peeling down the top of her flightsuit to tie the arms around her waist.

Her silhouette was clear against the backdrop of the open cargo ramp. As trim as her face implied, with curves that promised so much.

She's a flight officer in the 160th SOAR, man. You aren't supposed to notice that kind of shit.

She also had a heavenly scent of mountains in the fall. He'd grown up outside of Boulder, Colorado. How did a French beauty remind him so much of home?

He was tired enough that his reactions were wholly out of sync, he walked right into her when she stopped. He'd have plowed her to the deck if he hadn't grabbed her around the waist and kept them both upright.

But he'd also underestimated her reflexes for she saved herself with a step-and-turn that brought them face to face the moment before they pounded together.

# # #

Danielle's head rang with the aftermath of the hollow "clunk" that had resulted from their foreheads smacking together. The room…the Chinook's cargo bay spun for a moment. The three round windows to either side swirled and the square portals for the M134 miniguns—two forward and one aft beside the ramp—appeared to bob and swirl as she struggled to regain her equilibrium.

When she did, she became aware that she was holding tightly to the front of Major Napier's flightsuit. At least she'd tried to think of him that way; Pete made for far too intimate a sound inside her head.

Having a commanding officer tell you "you're gorgeous" was a fast flash of a path to hell. She'd learned long ago that if she didn't slam down the door, it led to unwanted gropes and casual caresses that made her want to both shower immediately—with a scrub brush and as much soap as possible—and break someone's arm. More than once she'd had to shove her M9 handgun down inside their belt and offered to caress their balls with a couple of 9mm rounds before they backed off.

So she'd slammed the door on "Monsieur Butler" and transformed him back into Major Napier. But for once she hadn't wanted to.

She'd just spent eight hours sitting shoulder to shoulder with one of the best pilots in the Night Stalkers. And when they hadn't been teasing each other, they'd both been stretching their tactical minds together.

One of his hands was on her hip and the other clamped hard at the small of her back holding her hard against him with such force it took her breath away.

"I'm," he leaned forward and took a deep breath with his nose buried in her hair, "really sure I'm supposed to say I'm sorry I ran into you." He breathed her in again. "But I'm finding it difficult to feel that way."

The last man who'd held her this tightly had earned a dishonorable discharge after she'd broken one of his feet and he'd almost broken her jaw with a massive punch before he collapsed to the floor. She'd used her Army boot to un-pretty his face but good.

But this time, the man wasn't the only one holding on. Pete had left his survival vest on the copilot's seat. Even through his flightsuit she could feel the strength of him. And also, that there was not a single thing to fear.

He hadn't groped her. Or gone for a kiss. He'd simply saved her from what would have probably been a painful fall onto the steel grating of the deck and then…wrapped his arms around her.

She managed to unfist her hands until they were lying flat on his chest. A part of her, the part that had found a mind that was her match for the last eight hours, wanted to haul him in and see just what kissing The Rapier would feel like.

But her common sense intruded and she pushed lightly against his chest.

He shifted backward. She could tell that it was reluctantly, but even in parting, those big hands of his took no advantage as they slid off her. In moments they were standing as closely as they'd been when they whacked foreheads, but now their only connection was her hands resting lightly on his chest.

"Awfully forward for a butler," she managed on a dry throat.

"Awfully forward under any conditions. But your web appears to have ensnared me."

"My web?" As if this was all her fault?

He took a half-step back, enough that she could remove her hands but didn't have to.

For the moment, she didn't.

"I am unused to beautiful, intelligent, competent women in uniform. Especially Spiderwomen."

Oh. Right. Her thinking was confused, so deeply *embrouillé* for her to have missed that reference.

Then he was gone, back into Major Napier and she lowered her hands. He bowed ever so slightly, stepped around her, and once more headed down the slope of the dim cargo bay.

The whole encounter had lasted perhaps ten seconds.

So why did it feel as if they had just moved past dating and meaningless sex right into courtship?

# # #

Pete had not just…

He couldn't have with…a fellow officer.

No. He hadn't. He hadn't grabbed her except to keep her from a fall. Hadn't brushed a finger across her brow to check for a bump where their foreheads had hit. His still throbbed, but when he rubbed at the spot, if felt more as if he was rubbing at the confusion within.

He had resisted the urge to dig his hands deep into that thick hair and bend down to see if she tasted anywhere near as good as she smelled.

He'd held her though. He could still feel her skin, the warmth separated from his palms by only a thin layer of cotton. The shape of her waist. It was easy to imagine how it would feel to be pressed against her, into her, plunging hard into pure heav—

Fellow female officer, goddamn it! He'd *never* crossed that line. Not once. He didn't understand how the mixed-gender teams did it. It was cruelty when someone like Danielle Delacroix…

Not fellow *female* officer. Fellow *officer*. Period.

One who had probably busted her ass twice as hard as any male officer to fly with the Night Stalkers. And he'd wager it was a nice ass even if he hadn't groped her to find out if…

Pete sighed with some relief when he reached the pale light at the foot of the Chinook's rear ramp. He was a goddamn wreck. He needed twenty-four hours sleep and then needed to get back to where he belonged—half a planet away from Captain Danielle Delacroix.

With that plan firmly in place he took the last step off the lowered ramp and out onto the pavement.

The breaking daylight slowly resolved faces as the crew chiefs chocked the wheels and tied down the rotors so that they didn't spin unexpectedly in the wind. At the moment it was only a gentle breath carrying the thick smells of Alabama, lush foliage soon to sweat with the intense humidity under burning skies.

The only thing missing were the sharp smells of engine exhaust and the piercing overtone of the kerosene in Jet A aviation fuel that usually floated around Fort Rucker mornings. They were far enough afield that there were only their birds, silent now except for the pings of cooling metal, and nature's, now beginning to awaken and call from the trees.

Already the Frisbee was in flight between the various crew members. Check a wheel, catch and wing off the disk, check the other wheel. It appeared to work for them, so he didn't comment.

There was a bright flash and roar from above as the flight crews finished up and gathered about him on the otherwise empty airfield. A descending blast of hot air sent the Frisbee tumbling aside.

In a blinding glare of white-hot jet exhaust, an AV-8B Harrier II Jump Jet descended out of the sky and landed on one of the nearby runways. The jet—with its vertical/short takeoff and landing capability—was one of the few fixed-wing aircraft that could land at Ech Heliport. Even a little private Cessna 172 would be hard pressed to get in and out of here.

Once down, the jet turned to taxi up to them. It was a two-seat trainer version and within moments of stopping, a man climbed down from the forward cockpit. He was barely clear before the jet was once again on the roll and lifting back into the sky with an earsplitting roar.

"Eight hours," Colonel Cass McDermott looked at his watch as he strolled up to them. "You're right on time, as I'd expect from Major Napier."

There was a collected round of gasps and exclamations from the flight crews that had gathered around when they discovered they'd flown the entire night with The Rapier in command.

"Damn straight, Colonel McDermott."

The sounds of surprise were cut off as they all snapped to attention and offered salutes.

"At ease," Cass offered one of his rare, wintry smiles as left boots stomped a half-step sideways and flightsuits rustled as hands were folded behind backs. "Relax people."

Again the shuffle as they shifted to as natural a stance as could be expected in front of Pete The Rapier and the regiment's commanding officer. Pete echoed McDermott's smile, but kept it between himself and his commander.

"Your assessment?" Cass prodded. "Or would you rather step aside to discuss it?"

"No need, Colonel. While unable to perform an in-depth analysis of each individual because of the situation, based solely on tonight's flight I would be proud to fly with any of these soldiers." Especially one, because, damn, Captain Danielle Delacroix was beyond good. So good that she'd managed to drag an entire class of trainees to excellence along with her.

"Good, because that's your new assignment."

He squinted at his commander. The morning light revealed nothing that would allow Pete to interpret this as a joke: foul, cruel, or otherwise.

Finding no answers there, he glanced over at Danielle. She offered a microscopic shrug of uncertainty.

# # #

Danielle had no idea what was going on, but Pete Napier wasn't looking happy about it. They were trainees. No one had told them if this was it. Was there more testing? Had they graduated?

If the latter, then they would receive their assignments and be dispersed among the five battalions wherever they were needed. With only ten graduates and twenty-four companies among the five battalions, they might none of them serve together.

That sent a surprising pang of regret through her. She might still be the loner of the crowd, but she'd come to know and appreciate the skills of Rafe and Julian and the others. She started being friends with Irish Patty and Rafe the Yank.

Though she had been hoping for the 5th Battalion D Company assignment. All of the previous women, who had become legends of the SOAR community, had ended up there. Chief Warrant Lola LaRue, Captain Casperson, Kee Stevenson the sniper, Sergeant Connie Davis the wizard mechanic and her giant of a husband…

Danielle turned slowly on her heel to face the two training crew chiefs who'd been along for the flight.

"Connie and Big John," she spoke aloud in her surprise.

"What?" Pete spun to follow her gaze. "No way."

They were the mythic mechanics of the entire 160th. Over half of all design changes sent to MD, Sikorsky, and Boeing factories originated with these two. They weren't just cross-platform mechanics, they'd as good as reinvented all three platforms between them.

They nodded in unison and offered her smiles. Connie's was slight and barely graced her quiet face. Big John's smile was large and brilliant in the morning light against his dark complexion.

The other crew members, even Patty, shuffled to open up a space around the two sergeants.

"Told you I had a couple ringers for you," Colonel McDermott sounded terribly pleased with himself.

This was like Babe Ruth and Willy Mays showing up on your T-ball team.

"I did it," Danielle couldn't believe it. "I really did it."

"Did what?" Pete was looking at her strangely.

"I," *really need to not speak my thoughts aloud,* "I made it. I flew with…" she waved a hand a little helplessly at Pete and the two mechanics. "I…" she looked at the rest of her fellow trainees and struggled to stop babbling. "We. Did it. We made it through SOAR training."

"Yes, you did, little Lady," the Colonel looked down at her. "Damn fine job the lot of you. You're all cleared as Fully Mission Qualified per unanimous agreement of the Instructor Pilots who have been making your lives hell these last two years and were watching this flight from a half dozen following craft. We've never had a team pull together like this one. I'm guessing that you'll be Pete's Number Two. Congratulations," McDermott held out a hand to Danielle who took it; though at the moment she wasn't sure what to do with it. The Colonel gave her hand a good shake and she did her best to reciprocate.

"The Rapier's Number Two what, sir?"

"Didn't he mention?" the man was clearly enjoying himself immensely. "Pete's forming up a new company, 5th Battalion E Company."

"What?" Pete spun back to face his commanding officer. "The hell you say."

McDermott didn't look the least perturbed at The Rapier's blast of anger. "Oh, did I forget to tell you, too?"

Chapter 4

Pete sat at the picnic table, or whatever meal you called it when you were eating hamburgers and chips at six a.m. after working all night. They were at a group of run-down wooden tables that were slowly decaying outside the Ech Heliport office building. A food truck along with a couple of Army cooks had pulled in alongside, fired up, and begun feeding them as daylight broke over the field.

Pete contemplated the situation. "How much trouble will I get in for murdering my commanding officer?" He ignored the sour expression on Cass' face. They'd known each other far too long for that look to scare him.

"Well," Danielle took a bite of her grilled chicken after cutting it neatly with a knife and fork.

He was so tired he doubted if he'd trust himself with such dangerous implements. Figures that she'd be beautiful. Beautiful. Shit, there was another problem. In the bright morning light, her Army-beige t-shirt displayed her figure magnificently—how good she'd felt in his arms for that moment hadn't been any kind of an illusion. Trim where she should be trim and rounded in such an ideal form that…that he should be taken out and shot. But that would have to wait until after he'd killed Cass McDermott.

"I think," Danielle continued after she was done chewing—good manners too. Hard to believe she'd been in the Army for seven years plus two in training. "It would depend if you intend to murder him *un petit peu*, a little bit, or kill him dead."

"Dead dead," Pete decided.

"Not my first choice," Cass commented as he sat back as if removing himself from the range of fire.

The morning had turned into a fine one and Pete had no interest in it, no more interest than he had in forming up a new company with a batch of newbies fresh out of training. And he wasn't going to admit to learning anything from them last night, no matter how much he had.

But he couldn't get away with that. The trainees had cooked up some ideas that, quite simply, *needed* to be added to training. And it wasn't just Delacroix. She'd given credit for each idea to the one who said it first, though it was clear that she'd been the spark behind every discussion.

"Court martial, *certainment*," she informed him placidly. "Life imprisonment, perhaps the firing squad?"

"Been shot enough as it is," Pete tried not to think about it. Four times in fifteen years of service, and his little brother who'd winged him when Pete had been trying to teach him how to hunt in the Colorado wilderness. His foot had been in a cast for months.

"No," Cass corrected her. "Firing squad is French, madame, or rather was."

"*Mademoiselle, s'il vous plaît.* And I am Québécois by heritage only. I grew up in Cleveland."

"*Excusez moi, mademoiselle.*"

To hell with Nicolai and his Russian, Cass made the French sound so smooth that Pete wished he'd studied that instead. He hadn't even made a study of French women who…he was not going to complete that thought.

The Colonel turned back to him. "If you kill me, Napier, I fear that hanging would be more traditionally appropriate if anyone has a yardarm handy. But come along, man, don't you want your own company?"

Pete tried to answer that one in the negative, unsure why he was fighting the bit so hard. The 5th Battalion was only five years old, based out of Joint Base Lewis-McChord in Tacoma, Washington. A through C Company were straightforward outfits—Black Hawk, Chinook, and Little Bird respectively.

Then Mark Henderson had formed up the 5D. He'd insisted on creating the only mixed company in the entire Regiment, all three craft types combined under a single command. He'd talked with Mark about it once when they were all sitting out a sandstorm at Bagram Airbase a couple years back.

"Mixed team allows me to be flexible on the fly. I don't have to wait for mission units to be called up from other companies. No questions about command precedence. My team. My training regimen. My orders."

And soon after their talk, "my wife" as well. He'd married the first woman to ever qualify for SOAR, and just like each woman who had followed, she'd done it by being exceptional. And when Henderson's wife had gotten pregnant, they'd dumped SOAR as if it didn't mean a goddamn thing. Pete shoved his plate aside and almost knocked his lemonade into Cass' lap.

Well, to hell with that shit. Any woman he fell for would have to accept she was stuck with a lifer for a husband. They were going to have to retire his ass into an old age home to get him out of the air.

Yet Henderson and Beale had flown together for a couple of years before that. Somehow the 5D was so far out on the edge that they allowed married couples aboard the various helos.

He glanced over at Connie and Big John seated at one of the picnic tables. They were from the 5D. Talk about an ideal match, the two best helicopter mechanics outside the factory—and better than most of those inside as well.

Maybe that's why McDermott had decided to let them serve together, because he couldn't afford to lose either one? Was that what was happening in the 5D? Was command allowing married couples serving in the same theater of operations to happen, perhaps as an isolated test? Had command learned that some pairs of people constituted a synergistic pairing that created more than the sum of their—

Shit! He was so tired he was getting all poetical.

"Choice is simple, Pete," Cass leaned in now and the tension went up at their table of three.

It rose far enough to focus all of Pete's waning consciousness back on his commander.

"You say no, I put these folks on their birds and kick them back to Fort Campbell for assignment. The units are hungry, we're getting pushed hard on a dozen fronts—as you know."

"Or?" Pete considered a mixed company of craft. It offered interesting possibilities. Of course a Night Stalker company was typically a dozen craft each. Though he'd heard the 5D was running with only seven or eight. The people sitting at the tables around him could crew just four birds. And that was only if he was allowed to keep Connie and John.

A couple of ringers for you, McDermott had said. Yes, they were here long-term if he said yes. Hell of an enticement to have direct access to two such skilled crew chiefs. But what bribe had he offered them to leave the 5D?

"Or," Cass pointed at the brand-new hangar behind him, "we can go look at what's inside there. But…" then he waited.

"And here comes the other shoe," Pete hated it when the other shoe dropped.

Still McDermott waited, but Pete couldn't get his mind around it.

"He must makes his choices," Danielle made her voice sound like Gollum from *The Hobbit* as she dropped the shoe for him, "before he goes in."

Oh.

"Yesss, he does, Precious."

Cass simply smiled as if such Gollum-speaking captains were completely normal.

Though Gollum with a French accent was distinctly strange.

"Good choice for a second in command, Pete. I approve."

Pete studied the crumbs that were all that was left of his hamburger. He was glad to see that his body had the good sense to eat even if he'd been too tired to be aware of it.

"No choice of personnel?" Pete didn't know if he was hoping for a yea or nay on that one. If he was smart, the first thing he'd do would be to reassign Captain Danielle Delacroix to anywhere else, as long as it was far away. He knew it wasn't merely exhaustion that made him want to drag her back into his arms. But it had to be his exhaustion that made that sound like any kind of a good idea.

The last time he'd been with a woman was on leave four months ago. Sally May Ketchum, as in Ketchum, Idaho, as in wealthy, tall, skier-athlete fit, and having no use for a soldier beyond a few nights' fling. Which had made her just about perfect.

Which is what he'd thought of Lucy, except she'd wanted marriage and he'd been young and dumb enough at the time to give it to her. Built, blond, as avaricious as a snake, and about as constant. He'd had her less than a year and it took him three to get rid of her.

Danielle Delacroix evoked none of the common logic that went with a choice like Sally Ketchum—the kind of woman best designed for a career soldier to enjoy and then move on. Nor was she a clinging, officer-hungry, conniving bitch. Danielle was made for cozy cottages and long winter nights. For whole long strings of them.

"No changes," McDermott insisted. "We haven't had a class like this one in years and I've been waiting for it. Part of that is thanks to you, missy. You may rest assured that I know that." He managed to deliver the line without sounding condescending. "That's why we held them together right through Basic Qualification and into advanced training."

Pete couldn't argue. Even after he'd "killed her off" her influence on the team's performance had been unquestionable.

"Perhaps you can change a few selected people later, but only by special petition directly to me. Also, every one of these people are security classified for the level of mission you have just returned from. Every single one."

Pete had to blink at that one. The Tibet mission had included only senior personnel with a minimum of five years in SOAR which meant at least twelve years in the service. If all of these people were cleared to that level, it meant that the 5E would not be a small shit-kicker outfit for long. They'd be capable of deployment where only the smallest, most flexible teams could go. For a bunch of rookies to have that in common, they'd have to have been…

He spun to study the faces of the crew at the other tables.

"Ah, the light goes on," Cass teased him.

"You started building this class two years ago," Pete accused him. The cooks and their food truck were gone, leaving a cooler of soft drinks and a platter of freshly grilled seconds and thirds if anyone was still hungry. Once again, the graduating crew, the two ringers, and the Colonel Cassius McDermott were the field's only occupants.

"Three years ago," the Colonel replied. "Right after you did the Myanmar mission. My whole plan for the 5E is based on the combination of you and Captain Delacroix, whose career I have been following for some time, even before I sent Captain Roberts to recruit her. Don't disappoint me, Napier."

The two of them? Cass had designed this company based on his and Danielle's skills.

Danielle was watching him carefully. Then she arched a single one of her fine eyebrows in question.

He was tired enough to stop fighting against his knee-jerk reactions and actually think. The chance at command, not merely of a single flight or mission but his own company. He had always groused at others' rules, things he'd always imagined he could do better. Now there would be the opportunity to try them out and see if he was right.

Captain Danielle Delacroix as his second in command. There was no question that she would fit perfectly into the role. She clearly respected the hierarchy of command, but also had plenty of ideas of her own. She would not merely push him, she would drive him to innovate.

That she was female and far too attractive wasn't her fault, even if it was his problem.

"Hey!" One of the Chief Warrants shouted; the redheaded female. She'd been fooling with her cell phone for a while. "There's a Mother Rucker Disc Golf course. C'mon you lame-os. I gotta need to kick some butt."

And just that fast the field emptied as crew and pilots piled into waiting vehicles and headed off to play. In moments there was only the three of them left. Even Connie and Big John had tagged along for the game.

Pete was too groggy to leave—oh, and his commander was sitting across from him waiting for the answer. Danielle was sticking close by his side.

"She would make an exceptional second officer," he admitted to McDermott.

At that Danielle hit him with another blast of her radiant smile. He refused to go weak in the knees over a woman, but he could feel himself smiling back at her despite his best intentions.

"Let's go see what I've gotten us into, Spiderwoman." He didn't even need to nod toward the hangar to explain that he'd just accepted the command of a brand new company.

The 5th Battalion E Company.

The first new company since Henderson's 5D formed almost six years ago.

The 5E.

He liked the sound of that.

She rose to her feet and headed for the hangar. Pete remained a moment longer at the table.

"Cass?" he said softly as soon as he was alone with the Colonel.

"What is it, Pete?"

"Remind me to beat the shit out of you some day."

"Sure thing," McDermott clambered to his feet and Pete followed suit. "Any particular reason?"

"Yeah," was all he said. Then he rose to follow Danielle Delacroix.

Pretty women were great, but they weren't exactly rare. Pretty women who turned him on had to have something special. In Sally Anne Ketchum's case it had been the competence of how she'd skied—the payoff there was that she'd flowed down that course the same way she had in bed—smooth and lithe.

Competence was a huge turn on.

And a challenge was always good. His best friend and girl-next-door Kim Waverly had challenged him throughout high school. Pushed him to always be better, to always excel. Had she been straight, he would have gladly skipped his family's tradition of military service in order to be with her. Both of them were first pick in every gym class, they'd captained several of the sports teams, co-captains in volleyball.

In the end they'd both signed on the same day…and her jet had been shot out of the sky four years later. They'd never slept together, but the woman's spirit had been a major turn on. Her personal preferences had led him to numerous cold showers and a whole string of bad choices, but he still appreciated every second of her short life.

Elegant Danielle Delacroix had the competence. And the drive. And something else that his brain, finally spent after making the decision to command, was wholly unable to process but he knew there was no way he could ever avoid.

# # #

Danielle had the lead toward the new hangar; perhaps a bit too overeager to see what was parked inside there.

So, she tried to slow down and look casually around. Ech Stagefield was like a dozen other practice fields, except this one was buried in trees and no other piece of Fort Rucker was close by. Only a narrow dirt road led from the sad office building toward the main fort.

And then the hangar. It could hold a half dozen helos, but she'd wager there were just four. Chinook, Black Hawk, and two Little Birds—had to be or their crew wouldn't fit.

That meant there was something extra special about these. Latest models? Some crazy tech mods—which would mean more training? Unheard of weapons? Or—

That's when the events of the last few minutes caught up with her and her foot caught on some unseen crack and sent her stumbling into the wall of the hangar. She spun around to check, but Pete and the Colonel were discussing something… and she'd bet it was her.

She'd been glad of the excuse to get away from the table, sitting that close to Pete Napier was doing strange things to her nervous system. Usually her thoughts didn't just slip out, like never. Yet everything seemed to around Pete. And her Gollum voice? She wasn't sure she'd ever used that aloud, never mind in public.

A little distance was a good thing.

He and Colonel McDermott had some history, long history by the sounds of it. She sure wasn't about to call the commander of the entire regiment "Cass."

It was only after the two of them were walking toward the hangar that she realized she wasn't going to get distance from The Rapier for some time to come. Had she really just gone from graduation exercise to second-in-command of SOAR's newest company?

That would be a "yes."

Was the commander Major Pete Napier?

Uh-huh.

Was she inexplicably attracted to the handsome man with: a reputation from hell, a calm manner in flight, and a wholly unexpected gentle smile?

Totally. She could still feel exactly where every finger had rested against her back and hip for the few instants that he'd held her.

You're in such trouble, girl.

His personal magnetism was making this woman's internal compass point Napier-ward. That was both disorienting and incredibly dangerous.

At the door, the Colonel keyed down the ten-digit lock code.

"Did you get it or do I have to repeat it?"

"Uh," Pete looked lost, probably too tired for his eyes to focus.

"I got it, sir." Every other digit of her personal cell number and the zip code of Fort Campbell backwards. "I'll bring The Rapier up to speed after he's slept." The Rapier. That was it. Keep some safe distance in her head.

The Colonel opened the door and led them inside.

# # #

Pete fumbled for a light switch and Danielle's gasp sounded close behind him. He himself was too shocked to make a noise.

For a moment, the room spun. Not because he had vertigo, but because what stood in front of them was so foreign that it made almost as little sense as finding alien spaceships in the hangar.

"*Merde!*" Danielle whispered so close beside him that he could feel her warm breath across his ear.

Chapter 5

*M*cDermott *was long gone.* And still The Rapier wandered back and forth among the four helicopters parked in the hangar.

Danielle had become even more fascinated by her new commander than by the four amazing machines.

She'd killed the big ceiling floods once the sun reached high enough to stream in the high windows. Plenty of light to navigate by; it left the hangar's interior filled with bright highlights and cool shadows.

Pete didn't *inspect* the vehicles of his new command—far too mild a term; he *prowled* them. His attention was worthy of a preflight by a post-battle mechanic's team checking every possible surface and control for damage. His eagerness was that of a ten-year old boy and a brand new train set. His power and beauty was—messing with her brain.

Danielle came to a stop long before Pete did and sat with her back against the main hangar doors. Ranged in front of her were four very unique craft.

She'd guessed right on the airframes: a Chinook, a Black Hawk, and two Little Birds; just as they'd flown in from Fort Campbell. But that's where the similarities stopped.

The Black Hawk was a DAP. The Direct Action Penetrator was the hammer-blow version of the Black Hawk—built and designed specifically for SOAR. The DAP Hawk bristled with the weapons and sensors that made it the most lethal helicopter ever built. It was sensitive in dozens of ways that were very bad if you were the enemy…and it was stealth-rigged.

The stealth transport Black Hawk that had been lost in bin Laden's compound had not been the end of the program, but apparently the start. This craft didn't look in the least bit jury-rigged, like the tail section left behind. This was one sleek, cohesive structure.

The two Little Birds had also been *stealthed.* The hull covered in reshaped forms of leading-edge composite materials. Even the weapons were encased in radar-deceiving pods, only their snouts peeking out through darkened holes.

But even more formidable than its three companions…

Danielle wished she'd chosen to sit somewhere else, but lacked the energy to move. She'd landed with her back against the hangar door directly in front of the massive Chinook. It was a wholly daunting piece of machinery that felt as if it was about to crush her.

Her Chinook…did she really get to say that? Her baby that rose so high above the smaller machines, was a work of the mechanic's art at its pinnacle. Every surface was reshaped so that radar sweeps would be reflected in unexpected directions. Unlike other Chinooks, the wheels could tuck up into wheel wells making the helo smooth-bottomed in flight. Instead of looking like the biggest street thug on the block, a little ungainly but wholly unstoppable, it looked downright nasty. She liked that in a helicopter.

Connie and John would go ape shit when they saw these helicopters. No, they'd stand aside and looked pleased with themselves. Of course, the two master mechanics of SOAR—who also had extensive forward combat experience as crew chiefs— would have been deeply involved in the designs of these craft.

No wonder they'd agreed to transfer from the 5D to the 5E. These four craft represented the very best of helicopter tech anywhere on the planet. Each time she looked at them, she identified another level of tech that she'd never used. ADAS cameras. Predictive terrain-following. A range of aircraft survivability equipment she'd never even known existed.

And all four aircraft were that elusive gray-black of stealth composite materials.

Stealth. That thought clearly hadn't sunk in yet.

Nor had it for Major Pete Napier. He'd done his survey in layers, she could see them building in his mind. First the walk-through noting what to study. Then the next layer to make sure he hadn't missed anything in the overwhelm of that first inspection. Then detailed systems study on the next lap…

And somewhere in there she had burned out and had to sit down to process what she'd seen.

But the man tired, beyond reason and tact, drove himself from 20mm cannon to heat shrouds on the engine exhaust ports. From fuel tank specs to Health and Usage Management Systems. She could feel him building up the layers in his mind as he studied and absorbed each helo's capabilities. And all Danielle could manage was to admire his relentless pursuit of that knowledge.

Eventually, when he was circling the craft—make that staggering around them—to no new purpose, she called to him.

"Stop already, Pete."

And as neatly as if she had indeed snipped the thread holding him up, he came over and slumped against the closed hangar door close beside her.

"Christ! What have I done?"

"What do you mean?"

He waved a hand at the assembled birds, "Look at them."

She couldn't look at anything else. The four fabulous machines, as in straight out of a fable, and the captivating man who had prowled among them for half an hour after she'd collapsed to the floor to watch him.

"You don't see it?" he sat so close that she could feel his body heat.

She looked back at the craft and it was as if his simple words had transformed them. These were not craft for training. Her days as a trainee were done. A SOAR pilot kept training through their whole careers—whenever they weren't actively deployed—but the Colonel had said "Fully Mission Qualified."

Colonel McDermott had said more. That being the 5E was an appropriate company designation, "Evaluate. You'll be responsible for receiving and testing the very latest equipment. That's how I convinced Connie and John to come join your merry band. You will always get new tech first."

Danielle blinked at the aircraft. So, they would be *evaluating equipment* that was out on the very *edge* of the *envelope*—a whole bunch of *Es*.

But now she saw what she'd missed.

The hardware defined the missions. Three lethal helos to protect the single workhorse Chinook. All stealth. These craft were for very high security missions. *High* security? Who was she fooling. That didn't begin to cover it.

"Now you see it. Bet you that none of the others will without being told. Damn but you're sharp, lady. That's very sexy by the way." He didn't apologize or try to take back those words. So natural that he'd missed them going by, even if she hadn't. He wasn't sexist, but he was by-god male. Looking the way he did, he'd have to be.

"These craft don't need testing," Danielle spoke in order to think about something other than the man seated so close beside her. "They're beautiful, state-of-the-art craft at the peak of development." As was the man.

Pete nodded.

"The 5E. E is for *Extreme!*"

His bark of laughter was appreciative, "Just like you. Danielle, the extreme Spiderwoman, Delacroix."

She'd hadn't just graduated into the 160th Special Operations Aviation Regiment (airborne); she'd graduated into the 5E. The 5th Battalion Extreme Company was going to be special even by Night Stalker standards. Once their team was up to the caliber of these helos, they were going to be assigned to places no one else *could* go. Tibet would be nothing compared to where these birds could fly undetected. Even the massive Chinook would have less radar signature than a standard six-foot drone.

Pete was still nodding, just a little dreamily. This close, his rich brown eyes were half lidded and he looked far less scary than he had before, standing in his skivvies while he'd been changing clothes. Was that only last evening? A dozen hours and forever ago. How could so much change so fast?

"You know something, Spiderwoman?"

"Many things," again she was teasing The Rapier, but it didn't feel dangerous anymore.

"I'm just tired enough to do something wholly inappropriate."

Danielle could feel all of her blood drain out of her brain. She had a very clear image of what that meant and she'd been fighting against the thought herself for some time. If he was less handsome. Or less competent. Or his reputation wasn't so sterling…

She took a deep breath and braced herself for the result of her next words.

"And what makes you think that it wouldn't be welcome?" Had she really just said that? To her new commanding officer? *To The Rapier!*

His eyes didn't widen in surprise. A man of action, he also didn't hesitate. Pete didn't go macho and grab her, he didn't try to dominate or control—which she'd been ready for. Instead, he turned and leaned in until their shoulders brushed the moment before their lips did.

The man might have a body and a reputation of steel, but his kiss offered a lush softness of surprising contrast and heat. Neither of them moved their hands. He didn't grab her breast, she didn't clutch his chest. Instead they simply explored the electricity that had been building all through the flight and the formation of the 5E.

At that she started to smile. It was small at first, but it kept growing until she interrupted their kiss with a laugh.

"What?" he whispered from a half breath away.

She shook her head and let some of her hair partially hide her face. He brushed it back behind her ear and she'd swear she could feel every line of his fingerprint along her skin as he did so. She was sitting on the floor of the 5E's hangar, her legs stretched out on the concrete that was still so fresh she could smell the dusty newness, and had just received a lovely kiss from a man she'd known less than a dozen hours.

"What?" he insisted with a smile that wholly belied his rough reputation. "As your new commanding officer I insist that you tell me."

The changes of the last twenty-four hours were just sufficiently overwhelming for her to set that aside. Commanding officer was a problem all on its own. For this one instant, they would stay in this idealized, non-military-code moment.

This time she didn't keep her hands off him when she kissed him again, but instead felt his need for a shave against her palms. Instead of heat, this touch was warm electricity, like a welcome shock that raced up her arm and straight into her pulse, amping it up higher and higher.

He rested one hand on her thigh as if he was merely steadying himself. It was neither suggestion nor possession, it was as natural as the kiss.

Pete sighed. It was a sigh of male self-satisfaction that had her smiling again. Moments later, he'd shifted until he was lying on the floor with his head on her thigh. And between one breath and the next—he was asleep.

Danielle marveled at the feel of it, the absolute rightness of it. When she felt the inclination to run her fingers through his collar-long dark hair, she didn't resist the temptation. She brushed it into an order of semblance that it resisted.

His face quieted, but didn't wholly clear. Even in sleep there was a hint of the frown of concentration that he wore so easily when awake.

She rested her other hand lightly on his shoulder and looked back up at the Chinook which had her centered in its sights. She couldn't wait to fly it.

To the finally silent hangar, still now from their inspections and from Pete's restless energy, Danielle whispered her answer to The Rapier's question regarding her smile and laugh. It didn't begin to cover what she was feeling, but it was the best she'd been able to find.

"It's been a good day."

# # #

Pete woke with his cheek warm on a woman's leg. There was no mistaking the texture, even through a flightsuit. Definitely a female's thigh.

He opened his eyes to the dim light of his new command's hangar. That thought was immediately clear…the woman's thigh was less so.

The concrete pressed unyielding against his left side, but he'd certainly slept in worse circumstances. Inches from his nose a sand-colored cotton t-shirt stretched tight across a very flat stomach and one of the nicest breasts he'd ever seen. He looked a little further afield, make that two of the nicest—

He must have jolted in his surprise, for Danielle woke up and looked down at him.

Danielle. He'd—Shit!

Her hair slid forward and masked her face in shadow, even this close he couldn't read her expression in the failing daylight.

But he could feel one hand resting lightly on his shoulder and the other tangled in his hair.

He tried to remember the last thing he'd done.

And then he did and wished he hadn't.

Please tell him that he hadn't gone and…*jackass. No games.* He'd just kissed an inferior officer under his command. That it had been mutual didn't make it any more right.

The last days had blurred together…*and that was another lame-ass excuse.*

"How long have I been asleep?" *Smooth Pete. Real damn smooth! Way to sweet talk someone who…who you really shouldn't be trying to sweet talk in the first place.*

"Long enough for my leg to be completely numb."

"Oh, sorry," he pushed upright and she hissed as blood flowed back into her leg.

She complained and twitched as he massaged it for her.

That set them both to laughing and he remembered her smile in the middle of last night's kiss. That led him to remembering the kiss itself and the sensual pull of her lips.

And using the excuse that he wasn't really awake yet, he was kissing that smile again. This wasn't some timid little testing like last night.

This time there was a roaring flash of heat that ignited deep within him and burned engine hot.

He knelt over both her legs and leaned down to drive their mouths together. He fisted his hand in her hair. He did it again and again to relish the feel of its soft depths slipping through his fingers.

His heart pounded with his need to have this woman, to take her beneath him. Here. Now!

The pounding increased and again Danielle's kiss shifted from welcome, to smile, and finally to silent laugh.

"What?" he demanded. This time he'd get an answer about why his kiss was so damn funny to her. She should be swooning, not laughing at him.

Danielle nodded toward the entry door to the hangar.

That's when Pete understood that the need pulsing through him wasn't the only source of the pounding. The first of the crew had arrived and, not having the entry keypad code, were pounding on the door to get someone's attention.

His attention.

But his attention, and his hand, were still lost in the texture of Danielle's magnificent hair. And his other hand was well on its way to ripping loose her t-shirt all on its own.

"Shit! Sorry. I'm so sorry," he pulled his hand out from under her t-shirt and made brushing motions at her hair. It seemed to fall pretty well into place. Mostly. A little.

Double shit. The woman looked like they'd really just had a long tumble. For a moment he considered ignoring the pounding, but that was even stupider.

That's when he noticed that: a) Danielle didn't look at all upset, and b) her own hands were up under his own t-shirt.

"Okay, mutual. Still really bad idea."

She looked down as she freed her hands and tucked his t-shirt back into the waistband of his trousers. Then she shooed him toward the door.

He arrived at the door, and glanced back just in time to see her disappear into the Chinook to buy herself a moment.

Pete blew out a relieved breath that she hadn't seemed upset. Then he *swore* that what had just occurred was absolutely *not ever* going to happen again.

He opened the door to see that most of the crew was already assembled.

Pete did his best to nod sagely at their varied gasps of awe at the four stealth helicopters they discovered waiting inside the hangar.

Moments later, a vision with dark flowing hair and a luminous smile swung into view around the Chinook. Never in his life had he seen a woman look even half that delectable and delightful.

"I know! Can you believe it?" Danielle perfectly covered her still slightly disheveled appearance with her excitement. "Come see! Come see!" She waved the crew forward from where they'd stumbled to a halt just over the threshold.

Beneath the rising tide of the crew's enthusiastic chatter he just hoped to god that he'd be able to keep his promise as a commander to never again put Captain Danielle Delacroix's career at risk again.

He was never again going to touch her!

And it was going to kill him.

Chapter 6

*C*olonel McDermott *settled in* the jump seat close behind the pilots' seats in the big Chinook.

"Haven't seen you in a month, Cass. What are you doing out here? Pentagon boring the shit out of you?" Pete knew he sounded more irritable than he felt. Or perhaps not. He was sick near to death with the training.

Not that it was wasted, the stealth aircraft had no operational differences from their more normal brethren, except that the wheels were retractable in flight, removing even that tiny bit of radar signature. The visual imaging systems were such an improvement over the standard that they were simplicity to adapt to.

But the helo's handling characteristics were quite different. Not enough to matter to most pilots, a world apart for a SOAR pilot. Reaction times had to be reworked, performance envelopes investigated and integrated into skill sets.

Even if he'd been stupid enough to break his self-promise not to touch Danielle, there wouldn't have been a chance.

Over the last month, Pete and Danielle had driven themselves and their team until the behavior characteristics of the stealth-modified birds were wholly incorporated into their nervous systems.

They'd flown tortuous courses throughout the lowlands over most of the East Coast, missions at the top of the Idaho Rockies, and spent the last week fighting war games back and forth across the Nevada Testing and Training Range.

The NTTR was five thousand square miles of convoluted desert terrain broken by deep canyons and abrupt mountains. With elevations ranging from four to ten thousand feet, they attacked various targets: mountain strongholds, anti-aircraft emplacements, simulated industrial and railroad targets, even mocked up cities.

But even inside the heavily protected boundaries of the NTTR, their birds were flown exclusively at night and were always under wraps by daybreak, inside hangars or beneath camouflage nets.

For a whole month Pete had managed not to touch Danielle Delacroix even once. They sat two feet apart in the cockpit every night and co-led the pre-mission briefings and the post-mission debriefings. They were perfectly cordial…and it was goddamn killing him.

He was actually glad to see the Colonel so that he could insist that Delacroix be transferred to any outfit, so long as it wasn't his, because he couldn't keep his hands off her much longer. He'd thought not touching Kim Waverly in high school had been a torture. Not dragging Danielle Delacroix into the nearest dark corner was agony.

He'd clearly hurt her when he clamped down the "steel barricades," but he'd had no idea how to explain or apologize. His reasons should be obvious.

And just to make him feel like a total shit, she'd responded by doing her damnedest to be the best flier and the best Number Two a commander could ask for.

"Got a surprise for you, Pete," he'd forgotten Colonel McDermott was even aboard.

"Great, just what I need." Pete and Danielle had gone through the startup procedures for tonight's flight with the smooth synchronicity born of fifty missions in thirty days. The pace had been exhausting for the crew, but it had left them with no doubt that they could handle whatever came their way.

"Typical time for a new company to hit effective-for-deployment status is—"

"Six months outside, three months inside." *Outside* being anyone who wasn't *inside* SOAR.

"And the record was seven weeks for Major Mark Henderson of the 5D."

Three more weeks. He could beat that.

"Thought I'd do a mid-training eval, see if you're even close," McDermott continued over the intercom as they finally began winding up the engines. "Can't wait to see what you folks can do."

The 5E team was so small that Pete had decided to be the Air Mission Commander from the copilot's seat of the Chinook. Danielle had proven that she was good enough to handle most of the flight tasks herself. That left him free to manage the strategic AMC role of directing the company in combat situations and still assist her as needed.

Dammit! If he pushed Delacroix off to a new assignment, he'd need two people to replace her. And that would shove him out of the copilot's seat. He didn't want to stop flying just because the woman beside him was so goddamn attractive.

Pay attention to your commander, Napier. Worry about the woman later.

"Engine Number One at a twenty-five percent rated compression," Danielle spoke.

"Roger. Engine Number Two start," he kept an eye on the oil pressure and thought about McDermott flying all the way to Nevada merely to "see what you folks can do." He had twenty-five companies totaling over two hundred craft and twenty-five hundred personnel. SEAL, Delta Force, The Activity, and Ranger commanders would be begging for every spare minute of his time.

People like him never just "dropped in."

Pete didn't want to do it, but he glanced over at Danielle. She was watching him. Her visor was still up so Pete could see that same fine eyebrow arch upward ever so expressively, just as it had that first flight back at Fort Campbell.

McDermott wasn't here to observe a training flight, he was here for a certification test. And that meant that McDermott needed the 5E to be ready—now.

"*Hundred percent* Rotor Rotations Per Minute on One and Two," Danielle announced. Her subtle emphasis let him know that she agreed with his assessment that they were a hundred percent ready for it.

"Oil pressure stable. Generator One and Two on," he threw the switches. *Bring it on McDermott!*

"Roger, APU Gen switch off."

Pete knew one other thing he was going to have to change in his plans. If McDermott needed the 5E to be ready now—for that must be why he was here—there was no way in hell Pete could afford to lose Captain Delacroix.

It didn't matter that having her remain so close at hand was going to cause him an insane amount of frustration. It was the best choice for the company.

He wasn't ready for how pleased he was that the choice had been taken out of his hands and she'd be forced to stay.

# # #

Danielle kept her thoughts to herself as she'd done since that first night in the hangar.

Finished with the Engine Startup Checklist, she buzzed through the Engine Ground Operation, Before Taxi, and Taxiing Check checklists.

She taxied forward from the hangar and out beneath the Nevada sky sparkling with the first stars and the last hint of gold at the desert horizon.

Despite the warm Nevada evening, she felt a shiver run up her spine; so strong it almost drove tears from her eyes—except she'd learned long ago to never show the tears. Never let them see you were afraid or hurt, never let her mother see how much every failure wounded. Cover it with a laugh—only inside her head, but still a laugh.

She'd been planning to ask for a transfer the next time she saw Colonel McDermott. Despite sitting in her dream helicopter doing what she loved, because she could feel the pain her presence was causing Pete. A month of flying together had done nothing to relieve the unbearable tension that had arisen between them.

Except when they flew. The way that man could fly…she couldn't get enough of it. And that perfect synchronicity in the air only fed her other, non-regulation thoughts, which didn't help matters in the slightest.

Most people who flew a Chinook thought that simply because it was such a massive bird, it needed a strong hand. The anti-torque foot pedals were indeed muscle builders. Some days after particularly long and stressful flights, she wondered if she was developing leg muscles like the Hulk. They'd certainly been weary enough to feel that way.

But the collective wanted a merely firm hand and the cyclic wanted its guiding French heroine to possess the light touch of a Juliette Binoche in *Chocolat*, not a kick-ass Carole Bouquet in Bond's *For Your Eyes Only*.

Pete understood the Chinook. His touch was as light and perfectly controlled as that single fingertip of his that she could still feel catching her hair and tucking it back behind her ear though the gesture was a month gone and there hadn't been so much as a tap on the shoulder since.

She couldn't blame Pete for standing back. It was his integrity that had slammed the door between them.

But it was a door she didn't want closed, even if they weren't supposed to open it. Danielle had considered approaching Connie Davis and asking how she and Sergeant John Wallace had managed to be married and to serve together.

But Connie was almost as terrifying as Pete. She lived and breathed the helicopters until Danielle wondered if the woman even *saw* her husband, though he was always beside her. And then Danielle would see the couple sitting quietly together over a meal, conversation whispered back and forth between them in a manner so intimate that it was impossible to imagine them as separate…and even more uncomfortable to interrupt.

That's what Danielle wanted. To feel that *merveilleux* connection.

Instead, she'd become convinced that the best thing she could do was leave the 5E and grant Pete his freedom from being so close beside her.

The Before Hover, Hover Check, and Before Takeoff checklists done, she lifted them into the night sky and turned toward the night's target range. The mission brief had been for a simple anti-tank op—

She twisted to the left and focused through the data on her visor to look at Pete.

He must have noticed her motion—or their thoughts had been so linked that he looked across at the same moment. In unison, they turned to look at McDermott and then back at each other.

The Colonel would not be aboard for a "simple anti-tank op."

Without a word, they both turned their attention back to their flight and their tactical display.

Tonight's flight was going to be about much more.

What would it be like to make love to a man with whom you were in such perfect sync? And why must she have that thought every time they were together?

Rather than risk even an encrypted transmission to the other helos in the flight—for the radio's energy output might give away their position even if their message was hidden—she performed a maneuver that she'd developed a few weeks ago.

Danielle spun the Chinook in a sharp three-sixty, like a spinning top, without slowing or veering from her flight path. It was a neat trick of maintaining speed and direction flying sideways, backwards, sideways, and finally forward again and had taken her several tries before her first success.

"What the hell?" McDermott hadn't been prepared, but she could feel Pete riding on the controls with her.

"We call it *l'étude regarde*," Danielle told him.

"*Étude?* That's Chopin or Beethoven or one of those guys."

"An *étude* is a musical composition developed specifically to practice a difficult technical skill. This purpose of this exercise is to *look* in all directions very quickly."

"But your helmet—"

"Does not," she was interrupting a Colonel, "tell everyone else in your group that tonight's flight is a trap and they must keep their eyes open."

"Did I say it was a trap?" The Colonel offered no hint of fake-innocence in his voice; he made it a cold, hard statement. As a commander of the 160th, she'd expect him to have perfect control like that.

"Get real, Cass," Pete spoke up.

The Colonel's harrumph didn't sound pleased.

"*L'étude regarde* is also useful if a rear camera is shot out and can no longer show on our helmet's display. That is why I originally developed it."

"You? Of course you. That's why I put you and Pete together. Knew you'd be a damned fine team. I want that trick submitted to the trainers by sundown tomorrow."

"Already done, sir," she informed him. And there went any chance of her transferring away from Pete.

# # #

The attack came as Pete was setting up the final tactical strike against the tank company out in the middle of the NTTR. His attention was mostly involved with the targeting information, and the occasional attack incoming from the tanks. Their shots weren't very accurate courtesy of the Chinook's stealth modifications, but they knew the 5E was out there somewhere and were firing simulated rounds at even the slightest hint.

He had Danielle do a quick reveal with the Chinook by nosing briefly up out of a canyon. It drew a series of shots from the six tanks. That in turn distracted the tanks from the double-pincer of two Little Birds attacking from one side and the Black Hawk from the other, while skimming only a few feet above the thorny brush of the Nevada desert.

But Pete had kept watching for the attack that hadn't materialized yet.

"Two o'clock high," Danielle's voice was a whisper against his ear. He'd been watching for it, but she'd spotted it first.

And then it was gone.

Once their sensors had a signal, it shouldn't be able to disappear again like that. Unless…

"We're not the only stealth craft here."

Danielle slammed the controls backward on the Chinook, diving backward into the canyon that they had departed only moments before.

A slice of laser light, passing mere feet beyond their rotor tips, simulated an attack through the heart of the dust cloud they had just left behind.

"All craft," he risked the radio. "Dance."

"Dance?" McDermott asked over the intercom.

"Shut up, Cass," Pete was enjoying himself. He shouldn't be. He'd just been attacked, insulted his commanding officer, and decided that he couldn't afford to lose the woman who was driving his libido nuts.

But he was feeling beyond good.

The 5E broke off their attack on the tanks, switching to their favorite dance moves. It would make them almost impossible to follow, especially as each bird's movement was different.

The two Little Birds'—now named *Leeloo* and *Linda*—pilots were fans of hip-hop and country respectively. The Black Hawk *Beatrix's* favored rock and roll. And Danielle flew the *Carrie-Anne* to Gregorian chant as far as he could tell.

They'd named all of the birds for action heroines—Pete completely suspected Danielle's hand behind it though he hadn't been able to prove anything—with the first letter matching the helo type.

Little Birds *Leeloo* and *Linda* from, respectively, *The Fifth Element* and Linda Hamilton in *Terminator Two*.

The Black Hawk was *Beatrix* after Uma Thurman in *Kill Bill*, a very hot heroine he had to admit.

And the Chinook was named for the best kick-ass helicopter-flying heroine of them all, Carrie-Anne Moss as Trinity in *The Matrix*.

"This is *Linda*," the Mighty Dozer's Little Bird broke radio silence. "Partial hit. Sim systems state that all weapons are offline. Patty is labeled as *copilot down*, which is ticking her off no end." Pete could hear her griping in the background; the system had switched off her microphone since she was technically dead.

"Roger, *Linda*. Get sideways and high. Give me some eyes on these people."

"Roger, *Carrie-Anne*."

"You have three birds on the attack."

Pete didn't recognize the voice, but they were on the 5E's encrypted frequency.

"Identify," he snapped back as Danielle dragged the *Carrie-Anne* sideways along a cliff face.

The voice proceeded to list their enemy's locations with no self-ID.

Beatrix called in, "Can confirm two of the three. One in sights."

"Take it out," Pete ordered.

"Direct hit," the unknown voice continued. Female, he finally had time to register the speaker as female.

The opposing "struck" helicopter turned on its running lights and headed out of the conflict. It was a stealth Little Bird. The other two craft turned out to be a second Little Bird and a stealth DAP Hawk just like their own.

It took twenty minutes—an impossibly long time in an aerial combat—during which they raced, dove, and dodged over the nighttime, nightmare landscape of the NTTR.

The terrain was a brutal enemy as well, providing protection and hiding places to both teams.

Danielle tucked under an overhanging cliff, her rotors spinning within meters of rock, but was able to surprise one of the opposing Little Birds.

The unknown voice interposed with data when it could grab some, which had proven to be reliable info when it came.

The DAP Hawks met time after time, their sophisticated targeting and attack avoidance systems making for such an equal contest that it was only after the 5E "killed" the other Little Bird that they were able to gang up on the opposing DAP Hawk and "kill" it.

By the time they were done, Pete was wrung out with the strain of coordinating the engagement. He'd led flights innumerable times, but it had never been *his* company. *His* people. It made all the difference in the world.

It cost them the partial loss of *Linda* and the complete loss of *Leeloo,* but they'd managed to defeat all three of the attacking craft.

While the final rounds of the aerial battle had been on-going, Danielle had used the distraction to work her way around behind the six M1 Abrams tanks.

The instant the last of the opponent rotorcraft was declared dead, Pete squawked, "Opening note!" over the radio. After all, their first objective in this crazy dance had been to take out the tank company.

Danielle punched on the full landing lights that should blind the tanks' night vision even as they spun their turrets to get an angle on the Chinook. But Danielle had slipped the *Carrie-Anne* into a gap between the second and third tanks so low that if they shot the helicopter, their shell was likely to pass right through the Chinook and hit one of the other tanks in the line.

When they tried to bring their smaller top-mounted M2 Browning and M240 machine guns to bear, Danielle's crew chiefs killed them with simulated hits from their vastly more powerful M134 miniguns.

While the tank operators were trying to unravel all the hell that the *Carrie-Anne* was unleashing on their heads, the Black Hawk *Beatrix* unleashed simulated Hellfire tank-buster missiles from their other side. The non-weaponized rockets struck each tank with a loud *klonk* that he could hear on the Chinook's external pickups. It must have really rattled the tank crews.

The war game computers declared all six tanks simultaneously disabled or destroyed.

"Back to Tonopah Airport," McDermott ordered. He sounded very pleased. As he damn well should have.

Pete however was still pissed at losing one helicopter and another damaged. Losing a person upset him, even if it was just a simulation; losing three was unacceptable. If only he'd somehow been better. Been able to…but he couldn't think of what he might have done differently; and neither had Danielle or she would have suggested it.

Pete found the thought a bit surprising. He was used to being the smartest man in the flight, always a step ahead. Danielle kept him moving, on his toes. He liked that more than he'd have thought; like missing a part of himself that he'd never noticed until someone pointed it out.

Danielle was that part; their flight operations simply fit together. He couldn't even tell anymore who had an idea first in a battle—their back and forth dynamic was that tight.

Cass had found him a great ally in his Second Officer.

Cass McDermott had also found him a good foe for this test; these people had been fantastic. That the 5E had won at all should be a victory even with the simulated losses.

"You just won the Kobayashi Maru," Danielle whispered over the intercom.

"What?" Pete spoke Japanese, but didn't know that. Perhaps it was Mandarin, but he knew that as well.

"The unwinnable scenario," Big John spoke up over the intercom in his deep voice. "You gotta catch up on your *Star Trek,* boss. Lady's got it right though. Sometimes you can't win the whole game. But the people you just beat? Oh brother, I didn't give us a snowball's chance. I'm so gonna be rubbing this in Tim's face for years. Years!" He was practically crowing with delight.

Tim? Pete decided it was better not to ask.

By the time they had flown back to the 5E's hangar he was glad he had on his helmet with his visor down and a breather mask in place to hide his expression. He was smiling, and he shouldn't be after losing personnel.

He'd fought them, watched them disappear right in the middle of a radar sweep, but he still wasn't prepared for what he saw waiting for him at the hangar.

The DAP Hawk and two Little Birds that his team had "killed" were lined up there—every one was a stealth configuration. How had he not known those birds even existed? Not so much as a whisper.

Yet Sergeant John Wallace, and presumably his wife, knew about these people—*not a snowball's chance of beating them.* That meant his crew had just beaten the 5th Battalion D Company.

Now Pete was definitely smiling.

They landed and ran through the shutdown in record time.

He did his best to school his expression as he stepped off the Chinook's rear ramp, but he wasn't having much luck.

Three women and five men awaited the members of the 5E on the tarmac outside the 5E's hangar, lit only by the soft wash of worklights from inside the hangar's open doors. They were lined up as if for a formal military review. The 5E formed up just as neatly in a line of respect.

The leader by the stealth DAP Hawk was tall with a long flow of mahogany hair; he'd met Lola Maloney of the 5D a few times. He'd heard enough of the others to identify the blond as Captain Casperson and the redhead would be the notorious Lieutenant Trisha O'Malley.

He also noted that the men who flew with them did not stand casually off to the side of their pilots, but instead stood close to their…spouses?

Two of them weren't dressed like SOAR. They were dressed like…he knew Delta Force operators when he saw them, he just didn't know what to make of the strange array. At least for tonight the 5D's two Little Birds flew with Delta operators at their side.

Rather than lining up with the rest of Pete's team, Big John walked up to the man standing beside Lola, wrapped him in a quick headlock and rapped his knuckles on the man's head, hard. The other man struggled, but no one moved to help him. In moments they were both laughing.

Pete had heard the 5D was different, followed its own rules, but confronting the reality was far more confusing than contemplating it from afar. Other than John and Tim, who must be the guy in the headlock, the two lines of fliers remained facing one another.

"Assessment, Maloney?" Colonel McDermott strode into the breech before Pete could figure out how to greet them after the recent air battle and defeat.

"Shee-it, sir," Lola Maloney offered a low New Orleans-accented drawl. "You entice away the best crew chiefs in the business and you expect me to happy when they kick my ass. Grumpy, sir. That's my official assessment. Very grumpy!"

"I meant your assessment of your opponents."

"Thought that's what I just said, sir. But I can repeat it for you if you'd like."

Pete had thought he was the only one who could get away with speaking to Colonel McDermott that way.

Lola stepped past the Colonel and came over to shake Pete's hand. "Damn fine job, Napier. Knew you and yours would be tough and we thought we were ready for it. Guess not. Damned fine."

Her grip was strong and he returned it gladly, "Anyone ever manages to take one and a half of my birds again, it had better be you. That was sensational flying, Chief Maloney."

"Climbing out of Pahute Alpha, how did you—"

"None of that now," McDermott cut them off. "Let's first get these birds tucked away then I'll let the chow truck out here."

# # #

Danielle was turning for her Chinook when she spotted a change that she'd missed earlier. Tucked close beside the hangar was a white shipping container with a set of radio antennas on the roof, big ones. Two women came out the door and then carefully closed and locked it behind them.

She recognized the voice of one of them as they approached across the grass that grew thick alongside the pavement.

"Pete," Danielle called just loudly enough to get his attention, but not the other crew members who were even now tucking the helos back into the hangar.

The two women had drawn close by the time Pete reached her side. Was he aware that he was standing as close to her as Connie and Big John usually stood, as the couples of the 5D had stood? No, because if he was, he would have shied off as he'd done dozens of times this last month.

"What is it?" She silenced him with a look and nodded to the two approaching women.

One was small with a straight fall of dark hair down her back. Her skin was olive-toned, her accent Brooklyn-Italian, and her walk like she was just daring someone to take her on.

Her uniform was military, even if her hair wasn't. Danielle, like many Night Stalkers, had taken advantage of the unique rules for Special Operations Forces, letting her hair grow longer like their SEAL and Delta customers. This woman had clearly decided to use that to her full advantage.

The other, the one she recognized, was a taller version of the first, except her hair, which swirled in great curls, stopped at her shoulders like Danielle's and her voice had the round tones of Spanish…no, Portuguese. Brazilian? At least in origin.

"*Ciao* and *Olá*," Danielle interrupted their intense debate about attack angles and flight endurance.

She'd nailed it when the women greeted her in Italian and Portuguese respectively; the Italian one continued over to the hangar confer with Lola Maloney.

"What?" Pete still didn't get it.

"Listen," she told Pete then turned back to the Brazilian woman who had remained behind with a soft smile on her full lips. "Please greet Major Napier, *por favor.*"

"Napier? *Maravilhoso!* I have heard so much of you. And now I have learned even more from how you fly," she pronounced *from* with a lush, round *frohm* sound. "You were better than I have even expected." Her words were a mellifluous flow that cascaded over Pete. It was the kind of voice that turned men into stunned puppies and it irritated Danielle that it looked to have done precisely that to The Rapier.

"Actually, Captain Delacroix was piloting the Chino…" Then Pete finally caught onto what was happening. "The voice," he focused on Danielle and nodded rather than turning back to the beautiful woman right away. That made Danielle feel a little better in a way that she decided was entirely too petty.

"Avenger pilot, Lieutenant Sofia Gracie, sir," the woman offered him a sharp salute which he returned even as he continued to face Danielle a moment longer before facing the woman. A Remotely Piloted Aircraft, as RPA pilots preferred them to be called. They became quite testy when you called their aircraft "drones."

"That explains it," Danielle confirmed. "We were wondering who was on our private frequency."

"*Si*. I helped you and Kara, she has the MQ-1C Gray Eagle, and she helped the others," pronounced *awthers*.

"Wait, did you say Avenger? I didn't know those were even deployed yet."

Sofia's smile was radiant. "There is only the one. I make Kara," she indicated the Brooklyn-Italian woman who had been with her, "so envious she almost cried. The Colonel McDermott sent me. He said it was a tryout. I hope I served you well."

Danielle had many trite images of how men might answer that statement from this tall, curvaceous beauty.

"An excellent audition, Lieutenant," Pete at least didn't appear to fall for the trap.

Sofia nodded and looked sad, "I am sorry that I do not see them sooner. It was only after you broke off the attack on the tanks that I see them. The stealth you all fly with, it is so very good. I am very happy my baby Avenger also has stealth. We must not let enemies have any."

Danielle hadn't seen a stealth drone…RPA, and couldn't wait. And the Avenger? High flying, long duration, and heavy equipment load, it was also the first jet-powered RPA in the entire American inventory—one of the most staggering pieces of hardware aloft.

She looked around for it, but there was no unmanned aircraft pulling up the hangar.

"Oh, they are still aloft. Our copilots," she waved a negligent hand back toward the white trailer of the ground control station, "they wanted to practice more together."

"Not just *Extreme*…" Pete offered Danielle a smile of acknowledgement despite the raw sexual power being exuded from so close at hand.

"E for *Extraordinary*," Danielle whispered.

"It is not him," Sofia faced Danielle squarely. "It was you that saw them first. I want to know how. How do you fly so *fantástico* and see them before me when you are supposed to be busy watching these tanks?"

Danielle shrugged uncertainly as Pete and Sofia inspected her, both waiting for an answer. "I saw something that didn't feel right," it was the best explanation she could find. The battlespace had been a gestalt, all the pieces as clear in her mind as on the inside of her visor. Nothing should have been changing outside of her primary target area, but it had.

"Oh," the woman leaned in and wrapped her in a surprisingly strong hug against her generously curved body. "You and I, we are going to become such good friends that I will someday know all of your secrets. You see if we do not."

Danielle had never been one to collect friends.

Pete was watching her with one of his unsmiling smiles that reached only his eyes, but shone from there. The man knew by now just exactly how much of an outsider Danielle really was.

Oddly after a month sitting side-by-side with Pete Napier, Danielle felt as if he knew her better than anyone she'd ever flown with. And she knew a lot about him and his family. Not a real close family, but absolutely a functioning unit; going through life together and supporting each other. She had tried to explain the luxury he had, but he still didn't see it. It was just a part of who he was.

And now he was laughing at her in his quiet way, because he knew Danielle made friends very slowly and still kept them at a distance even when she did.

"I'd like that," she turned back to Sofia. That would put him in his place. Besides, maybe it was time to stretch a bit and test out friendship—real friendship, not fellow-soldier acquaintances. She'd never find better people than the members of the 5E to start with.

"Of course you do," Sofia linked her arm through Danielle's. "We always need more friends. Come. We will eat together and leave this Major to dream of how much he wishes it was his arm and not mine linked with yours." And Sofia had her moving along.

Half horrified and half intrigued, Danielle tried to turn to see Pete's reaction.

"*Not* with the looking," Sofia whispered sharply and tugged on their joined arms to halt Danielle's turn to see. "You must make him wonder if I am crazy or if I am right. Do you know nothing about teasing men?"

Apparently not. And she didn't want to tease Pete. Of course that opened up the question of what she did want to do with him and she had no answer for that either.

She and Sofia chatted amiably about the flight as they headed back into the hangar to help the crew chiefs.

Danielle did sneak a quick look back at Pete when she was sure Sofia wasn't watching. He was still rooted to the grassy spot close beside the hanger where they had left him, still looking in their direction.

"He is still there?" Sofia asked while she appeared to be looking elsewhere.

"So much for being subtle."

"You can not fool a woman from Brazil. Not even when she comes to your country when she is turning into a teenager. It is in our blood."

"He is still there," Danielle reported dutifully.

"Good," Sofia nodded definitely and once more faced Danielle. "Then that is where you will find him tonight after all of us others are gone away. He will be on that exact spot, though he will not know it. Now, for rest of evening you will stay near women and we will all laugh together to make him even more out of his mind."

She wouldn't go to him. She wanted to go to him. Danielle did her best to hide her internal conflict and her surprise.

But Sofia's smile said that it was pointless to try and hide such things from a woman from Brazil.

Chapter 7

The practice engagement in the heart of the NTTR, for all its stress and ferocity had been brief. The celebration meal had once again been set out in front of the hangers except the lush heat of August in Alabama had given way to a cool September night in the arid Nevada desert.

After several hours, most of which he'd spent with Lola Maloney and Cass talking tactics—again Pete was reminded that Cass had flown his way to his position, not politicked it, because damn the man's brain was sharp—the members of the 5D headed aloft to fly back to Joint Base Lewis-McChord in Washington state before dawn. The area emptied as his team members headed for their beds in ones and twos; no desert disc golf course here and too tired even if there was. The last of them shrugged into jackets and left as Pete went to see McDermott off.

As they walked downfield toward Cass' waiting jet, McDermott again offered him an opportunity to change out personnel.

Pete bit on his tongue for a long moment before replying, "I…don't have a problem with any of them if you don't, sir."

"When was the last time you called me, sir, Pete?"

"Day you recruited me for SOAR, sir," he said it again just to mess with Cass.

The Colonel continued to move slowly toward a waiting jet.

"We need to change, Pete. In a lot of ways. I've given the 5D a lot of leeway in the past and they've performed. But Mark Henderson thought he was pulling the wool over my eyes on every operation. I don't need you to merely go out and be better than the 5D, they're already doing that—outperforming themselves every damn day. I lost Mark and Emily and assumed I'd have to rebuild the whole unit. But they trained Lola and she's added Trisha, Claudia, and others who are just as excellent in their own ways. They have two fully embedded D-boys to keep them on their toes."

Pete had forgotten to ask Lola Maloney about that. He liked the idea. Delta were some of their biggest customers. He'd need to think about the advantages of doing something like that himself. Once he'd seen what types of missions they drew, he'd figure out who to approach.

"I need you to go out and find the edge. That's why I'm glad you decided to keep Danielle. Every one of these people are very good, but she's as exceptional as a young punk 2nd Looey I hauled out of the Army National Guard a lifetime ago."

Pete kept his thoughts to himself about the lame kid he'd been back when then-Captain Cassius McDermott had told him he was being transferred to the 82nd Airborne and later to SOAR. Saying "no" to a fellow Coloradan hadn't been an option.

"You've never made me regret that decision."

"I won't let you down, Cass."

"I know that, you young idiot." Cass was all of six years older than he was. "You need to make sure that your people never regret signing aboard with you. You've run rough over a lot of people, Pete. There's gonna be a goddamn riot in my office when the others hear that I gave a new company to you. But I know what you can do. Don't run rough over these folks, Pete. They're yours. You're in big boy school now. Prove it."

"Yes, sir," Pete saluted.

"Not to me, you dolt. I already know what you've got in you or your sorry ass would still be parked in the Colorado Guard dinking around the sky in an aging UH-60 with a bunch of weekend warriors. Now prove it to them," he pointed back toward where the others had headed off to their barracks.

Then Cass climbed aboard his jet and was gone.

Pete wandered back toward the hangar. Stopped to look at the white control trailer for the Avenger RPA. Sofia Gracie was apparently one of his now.

He stood alone on the grass strip beside the sealed hangar that held the 5E.

His company.

It was three a.m. and the half moon was little more than a suggestion low in the western sky. The constellation Hercules was descending toward the western mountains as Perseus the Warrior began climbing over the eastern ones.

No birds in the desert, no spring peepers, not even any passing helos. The silence was so vast that a man could become lost in it.

"Hercules descends," he told the silent evening.

"Sent to his labors for murdering his wife and children while under the goddess Hera's spell of madness."

Danielle's voice was a body shock. He thought she'd gone with the others.

Pete couldn't turn to face her, though he could hear just how close she was—her voice had been little more than a whisper.

"And Perseus ascends…" he managed.

"…flying to meet and rescue his Andromeda."

"Danielle," still he didn't turn, though it cost him. "You should leave. We can't…" He couldn't finish the sentence.

"I know," she shushed him as softly as a kiss.

He wanted. He needed.

"How did the others…?" There was no need for him to explain what others. The couples of 5th Battalion D Company had been around them all night. As comfortable together as could be. Comfortable in front of their commanding officer who turned a blind eye. Perhaps because they were already married. The Army was changing, but not *that* fast. Not so much that he didn't recognize it or understand how—

Then she rested her fingertips ever so lightly against his back. The thin cotton of his t-shirt was warm enough for the evening, but not enough to fend off the heat of her touch. Hell, he'd feel the searing brand through full battle armor.

Her simple touch silenced all his careening thoughts.

"Tonight, we aren't here. Not the Major and the Captain, not Napier and Delacroix, not even The Rapier and Spiderwoman. There is only *tu et moi*."

# # #

The icy chill of Pete's unmoving silence made Danielle instantly regret taking Sofia's advice. But exactly as Sophia had predicted, he had returned to the same spot they had left him earlier, a mere shadow in the darkness of the night. The temptation had proved too much and she'd come to him—to be told to leave.

How could she have been stupid enough, for even a moment, to reach out for something she wanted.

There was only one thing she had ever wanted so deeply that it became a part of her: to fly. She'd been tempted to risk even that for this man, but still he didn't turn toward her. How had she read everything so wrong?

She let her hand drop. It was not for Danielle Delacroix to want things. She was the only child of an alcoholic mother and no father. Why had the gods made her want so much?

And now she had gone too far.

Would Pete even let her remain in the 5E? No. He would want her as far from him as possible, just as she had known he should.

Her fingertips were still warm with his heat as she turned toward the lonely road to base housing. There was only the one vehicle that had been left for Pete's use; she'd do her best to not give in to the tears on the long solo walk.

Danielle curled her hand into a fist to hold in the warmth at the same moment Pete grabbed her by the shoulders and spun her about. She inadvertently clipped his chin with the back of her fist; hard enough to knock back any normal man.

Pete Napier didn't react.

Didn't hesitate.

He pulled her in tight, trapping both of her arms between them, and crushed his mouth down on hers.

His voracious need surged over her.

She struggled for a breath, couldn't find it, didn't care, and leaned into the kiss.

Pete tore at her clothes and, as soon as her hands were free, she did the same to his. In moments they were mostly naked in the faint light of the sliver-thin moon. His shirt caught around one wrist and her khakis snarled on one ankle where the bootlace had knotted.

"I don't…" he gasped out as he drove her mad with his desperate grasps and grazing teeth.

She lifted the booted foot where her pants hung about one ankle, dug a foil packet out of the pocket, and shoved it into his palm. She had so hoped…

He had her down on the grass and drove into her faster than a DAP Hawk diving to the attack.

Their need let neither of them slow until the sensations rose too huge to contain and she released them into the night. Pete's moan was the bass note to her treble cry, the only sounds echoing down the dark length of the deserted airfield.

Chapter 8

I've," *Pete huffed out* the word and tried again. "I've never needed anyone so badly."

Danielle wrapped her legs around his hips and crossed her ankles. Her arms were locked about his neck so hard he couldn't have moved if there was an attack.

"I didn't," he'd kill himself if he had, "hurt you, did I?"

Her purr wasn't one of contentment but rather of triumphant declaration. He'd take that as a *no*. By the sounds she was making, an emphatic one.

He lay against her and only slowly became aware of other sensations around them. One of her feet crossed over his butt was still clad in pants and an Army boot, the sole of which was digging in hard. The long Nevada grass wasn't as soft as the lush Alabama grass of Fort Rucker. He'd imagined in a hundred fantasies bedding this woman outdoors on a lush soft bed of nature. This wasn't soft at all. Dry, scratchy, and embedded in hardpan soil with all the give of fifty-year old concrete. But he couldn't imagine moving just yet, not even to accommodate her comfort.

Pete noticed next how well they fit together and just how uninterested he was in moving. Her curves pressed against him and her Chinook-flying powerful legs wrapped around him. She shifted once or twice, but it wasn't in discomfort, it was to settle their hips closer together.

He'd never just *taken* a woman like this. Not in high school, not drunk in college. He might have paid less attention to a woman's pleasure than he should have at times, but he'd never simply needed to drive himself into one and declare that was where he belonged.

Pete spotted her discarded shirt off to the side. He gave them both a judicious roll that placed his back, at least most of it, on her shirt and shifted her off the itchy grass.

Ever since that first brush of lips a month ago he'd wondered what it would be like to make love to this woman. *You still don't know, Pete.*

"What don't you know?" her voice came out on a happy sigh.

"I'd, uh," *have to be more careful about thinking aloud,* "pictured our first time together differently."

"You pictured it?" No hint of disgust in her voice.

"Yes."

"How often?" No hint of coy either. Or of letting him off the hook anytime soon.

He tried to get enough distance to look at her face. But since her arms were still crossed behind his neck and he was lying on them and then the ground, he could neither move downward nor she upward. Despite the crick her arms were putting in his neck, he wasn't ready to release her yet. So they lay there speaking mouth to each others' ear.

"Often."

She did a thing with her hips that had him hissing with the sensations scorching up his body, and grinding his butt into the sharp grass.

"Very often," he amended.

"How?"

"How what? How have I fantasized about you?"

"Um-hm."

"No way am I answering that, woman."

She did the hip thing again.

"No way," he managed on a groan. "Spiderwoman going to bite off my head now?"

"That's praying mantises…mantis*i?*"

"I'm the one on the verge of death and you're conjugating verbs?"

"Plurals as in nouns, not tenses as in verbs. Conjugal rights? No, I didn't just say that."

He started to laugh. He was buried, uh, shaft deep in a woman and she was debating parts of speech. Well, not much debate from him really. She was *analyzing* parts of speech. And stumbling over words that meant marriage when they'd barely had sex. After what he'd just done to her, he'd let her off…this time.

And now he was thinking about word choices. *Fine job making her first time all screwed up.*

"No, you screwed *down*. Now that we've rolled over you could screw *up* though."

He tried thumping the back of his head against the ground to knock some sense into it but, with her arms still trapped there, it wasn't very effective.

Pete leaned upward enough for her to recover her arms. As soon as they were gone he missed them because he was a total fool.

"Danielle?"

"No. Don't go rational yet. There's plenty of time for that later. *Tu et moi.* We are all that exist in this moment."

"I don't speak French."

"Why not?"

"Because I speak Viet, Mandarin, Japanese, and—"

"What does that have to do with anything? A civilized man who is going to share my bed—"

"This isn't a bed."

"Never interrupt a French woman when she is lecturing you. If you had any manners you would *parles français* when you are inside her."

Damn but he really liked this woman.

She propped her forearms on his chest, rubbed her hand over it for a moment, and offered another purr of contentment despite her rant.

His hands, which he only now realized had remained firmly clamped on her butt as if it was somehow physically possible to force them closer together, traveled up from her waist and encountered her bra. He began searching for the release clasp.

"Hello. Sports bra." She reached down between them and tugged it off over her head flipping her hair across him in a soft caress of dark liquid that caught a thousand glints of the very last of the moonlight. Then she lay back down on him before he could test if her breasts' feel and shape matched the fine lines they'd made beneath her t-shirt. They did feel moderately fantastic where they pressed against his chest though, so it was hard to feel grumpy about the missed opportunity.

He stroked his thumbs along the soft skin to the sides. Even against his rough hands it was remarkably soft.

"Back to those fantasies, Mr. Napier."

"That's Major to you."

"You already did *major* to me. I'm just waiting for you to recover so that you can do more."

"Recover, huh?" He pushed her up until they were both standing on the grass. They stumbled about in the starlit darkness, doing their best to find their various pieces of clothing tossed among the grass. He would come back at first light to make sure they'd found everything.

Grabbing her hand, he led her into the dimly-lit interior of the hangar. Danielle stumbled along behind him, her one still-booted foot clomping loudly on the hangar's concrete floor. She turned for the Chinook, but he had something else in mind. For one thing, the pilots' seats in the MH-47 were almost six feet off the ground.

The DAP Hawk, a machine they both flew well, suited his purposes much better. A low seat and a wide-swinging door. Better yet, a Little Bird which had no door at all.

Before she could protest, he scooped her up in his arms and dropped her into the seat.

"Cold," she tried to climb back out of the seat.

"Stay."

When she again attempted to get out of the seat, he snapped the seat belt harness across her waist and pulled the strap tight to pin her there. He left off the dual shoulder harness as that would cover her breasts. They were very nice breasts, that perfect cross between perky and fullness, and he didn't want them hidden.

She crossed her arms there to achieve the same result.

He gently unfolded her arms, admired the shadowed view for a moment, and then leaned in to kiss her.

# # #

It was lovely. Danielle could do nothing but hold onto the flight controls where her hands had naturally landed as Pete kissed her.

Numb. Toast. Shorted out nervous system. She couldn't even raise her hand to investigate how incredible he felt or to trace the muscles of that truly exceptional chest of his.

Her grip tightened on the controls as his hands reached out to her. One dug into her hair offering her no escape from the lush kiss he offered, not that she wanted to miss a moment of it. Despite the almost violent heat of the possessive kiss, his other hand brushed downward more softly than a nighttime breeze.

Again she braced for him to grab and squeeze. Instead—twice as thrilling because he was so strong and his hands rough with hard work—he traced, caressed, and cradled. He gave the shape of her ribs just as much attention as he had her breast, and then—skipping the wide waist belt he'd pinned her with—her hip and thigh.

By the time he slid his hand up the inside of her thigh she was powerless to do anything but receive.

It was his fantasy. And it was so clear and so persuasive that she could make no effort to resist or assist; she could only receive. Her hands slid loosely off the controls as he drove her up until she was bucking against the restraint of the harness and his hand. Her ultimate release came on a sigh rather than a cry—a soft sigh of a woman she didn't recognize. She was always in careful control of her emotions, but around Pete she had no barriers, no internal gauge with neatly delineated areas of operation. He asked and she gave everything she had.

Danielle had never enjoyed dominance games, those power games that were so important to men.

For some reason that she couldn't identify, she knew that Pete Napier was not playing a dominance game on her. Instead, he was focused on giving all that he could to her in a place she so belonged, the cockpit of a helicopter. The pilot seat of a SOAR helicopter was a place that only a handful of women had ever sat, and she was one of them.

Pete was making love to her there out of all the possible places he could have chosen.

He acknowledged who she was and whatever trouble it would cause her—it was sure to be much trouble—and she loved him for it.

# # #

It was the sound of the tractor arriving outside the hangar that afternoon that had once again sent them scrambling for their respectability. Pete recognized the tractor's noise; it was a mower, a big one.

Definitely time to get moving if they didn't want to be caught. Somewhere in mid-morning Pete had finally bedded Danielle properly in the back of the Chinook upon a pile of folded-out rescue blankets, or rather she had bedded him. He had screwed *up,* and she had knelt over him and controlled his every sensation as she went *down* on him.

He liked the power of being on top, but the opportunity to caress and watch such an amazing woman as she slowly unraveled in the throes of passion and release had been incredible. The privacy of the shadowed interior of the helicopter had only added to the image.

They had then laid there together for the longest time afterward talking idly of nothing much at all. He couldn't recall a single one of the topics, far too aware of how Danielle felt lying against him. Of how protective he felt for the simple arm he kept wrapped about her waist. For the perfect contentment of her head on his shoulder and his cheek against her hair.

But the mower dragged them back to real life and they began tracking down their clothes. Some were in the Chinook with them, most were over by the Little Bird. A few other pieces were scattered about the hangar floor in places he didn't remember stopping during the night, Danielle's panties had ultimately ended up dangling from the long, phallic tip of the DAP Hawk's refueling probe for reasons neither of them could recall.

It was Danielle, not himself who identified his missing piece of apparel. No matter where they looked, he had no pants.

He sent the fully clothed Danielle out to check the grassy verge between the hangar and the flight control container for the Avenger RPA.

She made it two steps out the door and then turned back, closed the door, and fell laughing into his arms.

"What?"

"*Tes pantalons, monsieur.* They are now in teeny tiny pieces."

"He mowed them?" Pete pictured a thousand tiny bits of khaki scattered about the runway's grassy verge.

She nodded and burst out laughing again.

Thankfully, he had some gear in the small locker room at the back of the hangar, but it didn't help that Danielle's bright laughter followed him as he crossed the broad concrete floor in his underwear.

Chapter 9

*D*anielle *had thought they* were being discrete, until she saw Sofia's smile when everyone gathered at the base Mess Hall for breakfast that evening. The 5E's team suddenly felt overwhelming large. Two pilots times four aircraft, five crew chiefs, and now Sophia and her copilot, a quiet, blond woman.

She and Pete had slept little, but she felt simultaneously wide awake and languid. And she also felt as if everyone could see writ large on her face that she'd just spent hours participating in life-changing sex.

Pete was such a powerful personality that he was constantly overwhelming her. Her nerve endings were exhausted by the unprecedented scale and quality of messages they'd had to transmit. And her emotions were wrung from the degree of pleasure and joy they'd been forced to contemplate.

"Was it goodness, little sister?" Sofia asked in a private moment when they were shuffling their trays down the chow line together.

"Very much goodness," Danielle agreed.

"I knew this would be. The way he looks at you, I wish someone would look at me like that way."

"I think all men must look at you that way." Sophia's beauty was undeniable.

"Your Major Napier did not look at me so. This is how I know he is in love with you. Besides, when men look at me, they look at this," she brushed a negligent hand down her body in a move so graceful that Danielle could never hope to match it. "Not this," she tapped a finger against her heart.

Danielle had a soothing reply on her lips, but couldn't seem to complete the delivery.

Sophia's words "he is in love with you" had sunk in somewhere after dishing up bacon but before the scrambled eggs. The rest was a blur and she arrived at the table with bacon, green beans instead of hash browns, and a hot dog rather than the eggs she'd been looking forward to just moments earlier.

Orange juice instead of cranberry.

Hot chocolate instead of coffee.

She needed coffee. She caught herself only moments before she began dumping sugar into the hot chocolate, but couldn't seem to halt the addition of cream. Her brain knew it was wrong, but signals to her hand were not making it through.

"I'm...he's not."

"Who's not what?" Patty asked, the redheaded Chief Warrant, folding a long slice of steak into her mouth as she spoke. Her meal of steak and fries with a cup of soup made sense when Danielle looked at it. She looked at her own tray again and knew it was wrong but still couldn't quite get a handle on how. She was fairly sure that she despised hotdogs, about the only thing her mother had known how to cook, but even that thought didn't gain much traction in her whirling thoughts.

Sophia started to explain, but Danielle put up a hand.

"No. Don't you dare."

Sophia offered an elegant shrug and a teasing smile.

"I mean it. Violence will ensue," Danielle warned.

"You should not say such things to a woman from Brazil, my friend."

"Why not?" Danielle knew her voice was far too close to being a demand, but she didn't have control of it back yet.

Sophia simply looked down the table.

Danielle followed her gaze. The other three women of the 5E were seated close beside them and Danielle hadn't even noticed.

Patty was chewing her steak and watching her closely through narrowed blue eyes.

Sophia's copilot, Zoe who had emerged from the Avenger's Ground Control Station only after several hours of practice looked at Danielle in utter confusion.

Connie Davis' dark amber eyes were assessing, calculating. One thing that Danielle had learned about Connie over the last month was that there was a very sharp mind working beneath her placid exterior. She was a woman who observed and analyzed everything, even if she rarely spoke.

Connie hadn't missed what Sophia said, even if Patty had. But Connie hadn't been in line with them when Sophia had dropped the L-word. Still, somehow she's heard.

Or a worse scenario?

Like Sophia, perhaps Connie somehow just knew. Knew that Danielle was completely gone on her commanding officer Major Pete Napier. The over-serious, full-speed-ahead soldier—in addition to being the best pilot she'd ever flown with—was also the powerful lover who could not get enough of her. Or she of him.

And that they'd acted on that need. In the Army that wasn't a sin, it was a crime.

The odd thing was, the after-sex feeling was backwards. Usually there was initial attraction, getting to know each other a bit, sex, and then trying to ravel it together…which had always unraveled on her.

With Pete, they'd spent a month flying side by side and she knew him better than any man in her life…and then the sex. In a funny way, it was the flight test after they'd done all the training, which made much more sense when she thought about it that way. And the test had been passed with beyond flying colors.

"I find it interesting as well," Connie began. Her meal was a perfectly normal breakfast that she was eating very neatly. None of the foods were even touching each other on her plate.

Danielle longed to be Sue "Invisible Girl" Storm of the Fantastic Four and simply disappear, but the Spidey accolade had stuck so far—not that it helped, the requisite superpowers had yet to put in an appearance. It left her powerless to halt the conversation.

"We have integrated so rapidly with our equipment," Connie twisted the topic unexpectedly.

Was she being kind or merely exhibiting more of her typical mechanic's tunnel vision? Danielle couldn't tell by the expression on Connie's face. Either way, Danielle was thankful for the reprieve.

"I think that is your and Major Napier's effect. However, the 5th Battalion D Company had a higher level of personal cohesiveness by the time I had joined the company. Granted that was several years after its formation."

Danielle sipped her cream-dosed hot chocolate which was about the same as licking a stick of butter. "You're saying we're too unfriendly?" That didn't come out right at all. She and Pete had been entirely too friendly all day since the aerial combat test.

Her phrasing caused Sophia to smirk in a friendly-nudge sort of way that Patty still totally missed. Thank goodness.

"No." If Connie caught it, she ignored it and proceeded with a comforting forthrightness to answer the question at face value.

That was one of the things Danielle had learned about Connie over the last month, the woman was a straight-shooter who proceeded down a path until it was completely handled, and then moved to the next topic.

"I think that your focus on skills has been admirable. These are very unique craft that require a unique talent and last night proved that we have excelled. Beating Lola, Trisha, and Claudia. I agree with John, that was an exceptionally unlikely outcome despite your additional possession of the Chinook."

"*Your?*"

"Another factor to make my point," Connie continued calmly. "I should have said *our* without thinking, yet I didn't. Friendships have been very slow to form within the 5E. Powerful working relationships, yet. Friendships far less so in my observations."

"I'm...at a loss. I...don't know how to have friends." To hide her unease at such an unexpected revelation from herself, Danielle bit off a piece of her hot dog, unsure why she'd salted and peppered it. Because she'd thought it was eggs and hashbrowns? She discovered that she still despised hot dogs even with salt and pepper.

Connie eyed her for a long moment. And in that instant she knew that Connie was much the same. Danielle suddenly felt very close to the quiet mechanic. What had it cost her to leave the 5D? Had she had friends there?

"Well," Danielle gave up and shoved her unpalatable meal aside, keeping only the bacon and orange juice. If she was the senior officer here, aside from their commander, it was time she started acting like it. "Having our first meal together as the five women of the 5E seems like a good place to start, doesn't it?"

"Of course. It is a wonderful place of starting," Sophia bubbled.

Connie considered, glanced around the table, and then nodded once in simple agreement. There was a deeper meaning there, one that was terribly important to her.

Danielle could feel it herself. These women would be important to her. They would fly together, fight together, and become friends as only women in a combat zone could be. She had the tiniest glimpse of them being friends for life—which would have been an unimaginable horizon only moments before.

Patty was staring straight at Danielle.

"So, Pete was that good, huh?"

Danielle could feel the heat rushing to her face. He had been; more than good. All she could manage was a nod, but everyone's laughter made her feel as if she might actually belong somewhere. Maybe even right here.

# # #

"Do I even want to know what they're laughing about?" Pete hacked off another chunk of his steak and looked across at the four women. Damn but they were a sight. And Danielle…shit! The woman glowed among them. He'd wrung out both of their bodies and he could feel himself hardening anyway with his need to do it all over again.

"Nope," Big John rumbled out. "You can trust me on that. You really don't want to know."

"Who's the chick again?" Mickey "The Mighty Dozer" Quinn asked. The man fit his name. He was a big Alaskan native, not as big as Big John, but close. Pete felt small sitting at the table with the two of them.

"That chick is my wife," Big John rumbled out, but after a month of flying together there was no question of Dozer referring to Connie.

"Lieutenant Sophia Gracie is an Avenger pilot. The 5E gets a dedicated stealth drone and she's the one flying it." He recognized the look in Dozer's eyes. "And don't even think about it." Of course his own thoughts were plenty preoccupied.

Dozer flinched and looked at him, "Right. Sorry, sir."

Big John slapped Pete on the back so hard he was glad his elbows were on the table or he'd have face-planted in his steak.

Pete decided that if he didn't want to know what was making the women laugh, and ten times as much he didn't want to know what so amused Big John.

# # #

Danielle finally broke down and went back for a proper breakfast. She thought up a topic change on her way back to the table. She *needed* a topic change. The way Pete's eyes tracked her to the chow line and back sent prickles up her skin.

Sophia might say he loved her, but that wasn't on either of their rosters. Though she and Pete certainly needed each other; there had *never* been sex like his anywhere in her experience. The raw force of his personality had battered at her until she could only hang on and go for the ride he'd taken her on…but, oh my god, what a ride! She couldn't wait to climb aboard again.

She carefully didn't look at Pete though he was only two tables away.

"Good girl," Sophia whispered to her as she sat back down. The woman's wink was sly and friendly. Pete was back over Danielle's right shoulder, but thankfully the women were to her left so she could avoid constantly glancing over at him.

"Your Avenger," Danielle went for her topic change, "it needs a name."

"It's a drone, so we could name it *Danielle* for being a force of nature," Patty suggested. "No. Wait. We already have one of those." This time the laughter around the table was friendly and Danielle could feel herself melting. She was no longer standing off to the side observing; instead she was participating. Welcome. Maybe even wanted.

"Or *Dorothy* for killing the Wicked Witch of the West," Connie put in. "Though it was technically her house that did the work, probably suffering severe damage to its foundation. That always bothered me as a child, Dorothy gets the credit, but it is the house that—"

"My baby, she is no *drone*. She is an RPA. Remotely Piloted Aircraft and I am her pilot." Sophia sat bolt upright, fists on her hips and her dauntingly curvaceous chest thrust forward in defiance.

"*Ripley* for Sigourney in *Alien?*" Zoe jumped in with no fear despite being new to the group.

"*Robin* for Mrs. Robinson from *The Graduate.*"

"No! My Avenger is very sexy and very dangerous, but not evil. *Absolutamente não!*" She held up a palm for emphasis.

"*Raider* for *Raiders of the Lost Ark?*"

"Hello, female heroine rule, remember?" Danielle put in. She was rather proud of slipping that rule past Pete without his noticing until after all his birds were named.

"Or *Raven* for Marion Ravenwood in *Raiders?*" Zoe again, with a shy smile that bothered offered and welcomed. Danielle had liked her at first meeting last night, and even more so now. She was a good addition to their team.

"Ooo," Sophia purred, "that one it is right. She keeps Indy in his place, does she not?"

"*Ms. Raven* it is," Danielle declared.

And she finally allowed herself to glance over her shoulder at Pete. He might be a powerful force, but her new friends had dubbed her a *force de la nature.* She was Spiderwoman. The Number Two of SOAR's newest company. Befriended of four pretty damn impressive women.

And in that moment Danielle knew what she wanted.

Yes, Pete, she thought to herself. *I too am powerful. You had best be ready for me.*

She offered him her blandest smile before turning back to her friends. This time Sophia offered no wink and Patty no smirk.

But beneath the edge of the table, Connie briefly squeezed her hand in acknowledgement.

Yes, now she understood Connie and Big John.

Danielle knew what she wanted. And it wasn't just for another amazing tumble among the helicopters.

Patty started some story about a gunnery sergeant who thought he could outshoot her. But Patty was a girl raised hunting duck in late summer and deer, moose, and bear with her grandda each Thanksgiving vacation in the woods of Maine. Apparently the gunny had then tried to out-cuss her, but Patty had also grown up playing on the fishing docks of Gloucester throughout the school year.

After being with Pete Napier, Danielle knew she was done hunting. She didn't want anyone else. Ever.

# # #

"Major Pete Napier?" a cute blond orderly appeared next to Dozer. The man hooked a thumb toward Pete.

She gave Pete a pert salute, and a radiant smile that his face typically earned him. She handed him a sealed envelope and, when he did no more than salute back, she was gone. It was hard not to admire her loose-hipped walk, but all it made him think of was Danielle's unselfconscious elegance.

Danielle's walk wasn't a tease, nor a declaration of power like Sophie's sensuously confident stride. Danielle's walk spoke simply and clearly, here is a woman eminently sure of herself. No need to entice, she was simply, wholly herself.

It was the same startling way she made love. She gave as freely as she took. Not submissive, but as an equal. He'd never forget that first time when he'd taken her with blinding, unthinking-animal need, and she was the one who had sounded triumphant afterward. Whereas he'd been shattered; a thousand shards scattered at her feet in supplication hoping she would grant him more. And she had.

"You gonna do something with that?"

Pete glared at Dozer and wondered how the hell the man knew about himself and Danielle.

Then he noticed that the man was looking at the sealed orders Pete was still holding.

As he started to tear it open, Big John's hard elbow slammed into his ribs. As Pete jerked in surprise, and grunted hard at the force of the blow, he tore the envelope and the orders in half.

He pulled out the two pieces of paper and slid them together so that he could read across the tear.

Big John leaned over his shoulder to read and offered a low whistle.

"What?" Dozer leaned in trying to read them upside down from across the table.

"The 5E is declared active and ready for deployment," Pete finally managed.

"Hot damn!" Dozer and John high-fived across the table.

Pete scanned the rest, rising to his feet as he did so. He barely heard their questions trailing after him.

He moved up beside Danielle, interrupted something that had them all laughing again: Patty's guffaw, Sophia's laugh, Connie and Zoe's quiet smiles, and Danielle's near giggle. He handed her the orders.

"Is there a reason that you have torn these in half?" she teased him as she began reading. She stopped after the first line and turned to face the other women. "We have done it. We are declared ready."

"Wow!" "In four weeks?" "That is so excellent!"

"Thank you," Danielle sounded so sincere to her crew that Pete felt like an idiot. He'd never for a moment thought about thanking John and Dozer even though it was as much their doing as his.

"Keep reading," he prompted her.

She did and then looked up at him wide-eyed. At his nod, she turned back to her companions, "Time to saddle up, ladies. First mission starts now. Hope you like sushi."

And that fast, Danielle had her people moving. She didn't even have to call out to the other tables where the crew were scattered and chatting over their finished meals. The women of the 5E were in motion? Then the whole company followed.

He finally began to understand the advantages of having women in the field for more than the immense competence they had shown him over the last month.

Moving as a true unit for the first time, the men and women of the 5E dumped their trays at the dishwasher's window and formed up loosely to follow him to the hangars.

Of course, even though they were side by side, he wasn't so sure that he and the others weren't actually following Danielle.

Chapter 10

S*ix hours it took* to break down the helicopters far enough to fit into a C-5 Galaxy transport," John moaned as he finished the last inspection on the reassembled Chinook helicopter now parked in a secure hangar at Kadena Air Base in Okinawa, Japan.

Pete agreed, it was always a long, pain-in-the-ass process to move a big bird like the Chinook across long distances. A couple thousand miles was no real problem, the sixty-five hundred miles from the NTTR to Japan, was a whole different matter. They could do it, in a forty-hour flight with multiple mid-air refuelings over the open ocean…it was easier and safer to take it apart enough to stuff it on an Air Force jet.

The hangar, not as new as the one at Mother Rucker or as dusty and dry as the one at the Nevada Range, was still similar enough that Pete found it to be terribly disorienting.

Their scenery had been an exchange from an arid desert airbase in the dead of night to a hot, tropical airbase in the dead of night.

He'd served a lot of time here in Japan, frequently flying into Korean and Russian airspace. But inside the hangar he was in some weird bubble of technology, surrounded by four helicopters he still wasn't used to seeing, and the crew he was still getting to know, though he'd learned to totally trust.

"It's because you're on the goddamn Chinook," Patty was teasing John. "My Little Bird was ready in fifteen minutes."

"Pipsqueak little machine," John said bitterly but with no malice in his tone that Pete could detect.

It wasn't really fair. For transport on the massive C-5 Galaxy transport jet, the Little Bird only needed to have the fuel tanks drained and then fold the rotor blades back until they hung over the tail. On the Chinook, it was necessary to remove not only the six massive rotor blades, but also tear down the rotor heads as well.

Pete was impressed as hell that they'd done it in only six hours because the stealth modification added a lot of shapes and layers around the normal, large-to-begin-with rotor heads.

"Then twelve hours in transit aboard a roaring steel can," Rafe whined continuing the chronicle of the last twenty-four hours.

"Run by the U.S. Air Farce," Julian tossed in. The Air Force had command of all of the big transports.

"And Connie took us all for way too much money at poker," Pete decided it was time to shift the mood of the crew.

"That's my gal," John was suddenly beaming. "Of course if she shared her winnings instead of taking my money too I might be happier." The game had raged for hours over the Pacific, and Connie was the winner by a wide margin.

It was clear that John couldn't be prouder. And Pete half suspected that Connie's winnings would find their way back to John at vacation time or perhaps as a surprise savings account at their retirement. Connie didn't seem like a gal into frills, glad as could be to serve in the Army and let the military provide the basics.

"Took you seven hours to rebuild the Chinook," Pete decided maybe John didn't deserve to be both happy *and* have a loving wife like Connie.

John groaned once again, "Don't remind me."

Deserve. Did Pete deserve a woman like Danielle? Wow! There was a loaded question. Did he feel like the luckiest shit on the planet for getting to bed her? Oh yeah.

But what had he done to deserve her attentions? That was far less clear. He'd been consistently grouchy about forming the 5E, then driving everyone like mad to excel because of *his* desire to get back in the field.

"Why are you even with me?"

"Cause you're the boss," Big John thumped him on the shoulder.

Pete definitely needed his head examined, perhaps starting with a swift smack. He looked around for Danielle and instead spotted a team of four men who entered and crossed the hangar floor with the smooth grace of top operators.

One moved like an officer despite his big pack. The other three were also humping packs, even bigger ones. Two of the three had beards and civilian hair. The third was clean-shaven…no, another woman in the service. They were everywhere all of a sudden.

"Hi Pete," Lieutenant Commander Luke Altman came up and shook his hand; a crushing grip that Pete gladly returned.

"Hey Luke," he'd carried LCDR Altman and his SEAL teams on any number of missions. Altman was one of the very best the Navy had to offer. "What brings a bunch of SEALs to Okinawa?"

"You do."

Pete gave himself a moment to digest that. They'd had the choppers together for about seven minutes and, *ding*, on cue, in come the operators. He could feel Cass McDermott back there pulling strings.

Luke dropped his pack to the concrete floor and the other three did the same.

"Didn't know you had women in the SEALs." Pete bought himself another moment to consider things.

If Luke was involved, this op went way higher up the pecking order than just Cass. Joint Special Operations Command was in on this one.

"No offense intended, ma'am," he addressed the woman. After all, it didn't pay to tick off a Navy SEAL.

"I have Nikita," Luke shrugged "Night Stalkers have…" Luke looked him up and down, "you! No offense intended Nikita."

She simply rolled her eyes at her commander's back.

"I felt that," Luke said without bothering to turn to her.

It was the sworn duty of every service member to look down on anyone in another branch. Pete opened his mouth to say something about having learned how to be a wimp by watching SEALs—

"Are you now one of the women of SOAR, Major Napier?" Danielle appeared at his elbow as if magically transported.

It was unnerving how easily she did that to him. She was the only person who could slip past his situational awareness. The woman he should be most sensitive to, and she did it to him constantly.

"You must be very proud to be one of us. Do you wear a dress often?"

"No. Do you?" Pete shot back at her.

"Only when someone takes me dancing."

"Lady," Luke grinned at her with a lascivious smile and Pete resisted a sudden urge to flatten the SEAL commander up against the side of the DAP Hawk parked close behind him, "if I weren't already married, that would be a date. What about you, Pete?"

"Me? Do I look like I dance?"

"I don't know. Grass skirt, a couple white orchid Hawaiian leis. I think you'd make a picture."

"Don't forget the ukulele," Danielle was being of no help at all.

"Would you dance with a man if he played the ukulele?"

Danielle looked at Pete as if she was trying on the picture for size. A smile teased along the edge of her lips. He knew what that smile felt like when he was kissing her back at the NTTR, but he'd never seen it before.

He'd hadn't seen this smile because for a month he'd kept her at arm's length and ignored the pain he'd caused them both by refusing to even acknowledge their one kiss. And now he'd done a hell of a lot more than kissed her and it was one of the best things to ever happen to him.

Unlike the radiant blast of her "happy smile"—which made her beyond gorgeous—this one made her impossibly cute.

"Hard to imagine, isn't it?" Luke said. "Loving anyone who plays a ukulele."

"Hard enough to imagine even dancing with one," she admitted.

"I. Don't. *Play!* The ukulele."

Danielle ignored him and turned back to Luke. "He also said he doesn't dance, should we trust him on that?"

"Pete's always been more of a tromp on 'em and leave 'em kind of guy."

"Shut up, Luke. Or I'll be telling stories on you that'll burn your team's ears."

"Hell, Pete. You can't threaten a SEAL and expect to be left alive."

"Sir," Nikita spoke up for the first time. "I think you said that we need him for this mission. Won't be much use to us dead. Perhaps we can kill him for you afterward?" Her voice was mission-asset deadpan.

"See why I keep her around?" Luke snapped his fingers and pointed at an open spot of floor next to him.

# # #

Danielle didn't have to wonder what the signal meant for long. In moments the other SEALs had grabbed a fold-up table from where it leaned against the hangar's wall and set it up where Luke had pointed.

He reached into his pack and pulled out a long map tube. Nikita had a worklight plugged in and moved over. All of the

Night Stalkers gathered around the table as the SEAL commander rolled out the map. The SEALs dropped into a line standing at ease behind their commander, like a personal body guard.

Danielle tried to look at them without looking. She'd flown with a few Delta operators, they tended to be smaller men. Whatever Delta's selection process was, it favored lean, whip-strong men of average height.

The SEAL commander and the two men topped six feet and Nikita wasn't far behind them. They stood at ease, but looked lethal. You could look at a Delta and wonder what his day job was. You looked at a SEAL and they exuded power and physical conditioning. Even their loose camo pants couldn't hide the powerful swimmer's legs. There was never a question about what a SEAL did for a living.

Standing safe in a friendly hangar, the Night Stalkers still all wore their sidearms. The SEALs had that plus massive knives strapped to their thighs. Another at the ankle. Their rifles were not strapped to their packs; rather they'd carried them in, and only rested them against their packs close to hand. She felt safer simply for having them here.

Then she looked down at the map.

"Uh, that's China. Or at least a part of it."

"Is it?" the Lieutenant Commander stared down at it in shock. "Well, I'll be damned. You're right, little lady. Pete, you should definitely take this lady out dancing. Though she's smart, so maybe not your type. Unlike Brittany or Lucy or—"

"Eat hot shit, Luke!" Pete's growl spoke of a long friendship.

So Pete liked them dumb? Yet he certainly seemed to like her. This would *assurément* be an interesting ride.

Time for a subject change.

"China?"

"Yes," Luke threw some internal switch and became all business. "The Jiangnan Shipyard is China's premier large ship-builder. They are presently building a pair of the world's largest Coast Guard ships." He tossed down several large glossy photos.

She knew enough about ships to know it was big, but not much more.

"Three times more displacement than our largest—if you don't count our two broken down ice breakers. Fifty percent bigger than our destroyers and missile cruisers. The only thing we still have that have greater displacement are our helicopter and aircraft carriers."

"So," Patty pointed a finger at the image, "you're saying these things are big?"

Pete rolled his eyes, but Luke nodded matter of factly.

"Big and heavily armed," and he listed off an impressive array of armament. "She also carries a pair of Chinese Z-8 helicopters."

That got everyone's attention. Night Stalkers might not be impressed by deck-mounted guns on a ship no matter their number or size. But the Z-8 was a heavy lifter. It could move a lot of troops quickly and even mount missiles; a far more formidable opponent than the Augusta Westlands that served on U.S. Coast Guard ships.

"What do you do with a Coast Guard ship that big?" Rafe was a good strategy man, which made him ideal as the DAP Hawk pilot.

"The Chinese are dredging sediment and then building man-made islands on top of submerged reefs in Vietnamese and Philippine waters, an area called the Spratly Islands. They're building military bases on them, seven hundred miles from their mainland. You can't protect those without a Coast Guard ship that can cruise for a long time and bring some serious firepower to guard them."

"And we're supposed to do something about them?"

Luke looked at her for a long moment before replying, "We didn't come to Japan for the sushi."

No, they hadn't.

Chapter 11

*T*hey had twenty-four hours off, between the completion of the mission plan and launch.

A day and a night.

Not a chance was Pete going to waste that in a barracks bunk and eating in an American chow hall, not when Japan beckoned.

Nor was he going to do it alone.

He commandeered a car from the motor pool shortly after sunrise—managed not to look like an idiot by remembering just in time that Japan was a right-hand drive country. Nothing fancy, just a blah-green Toyota sedan.

When Danielle came out to the car, he wished he'd found a Miata convertible or a Honda S2000. She wasn't a Ferrari sort of woman, but she definitely evoked the need for a convertible where the wind could play with her hair.

She shouldn't appear so startling to him, after all they'd rarely been apart in the entire last month of training. But it was the first time he'd seen her in civilian clothes. Sneakers, form-hugging jeans, and a nice, simple blouse should not be such a shock, but they were. The nondescript knapsack over one shoulder and dark wrap-around shades only completed the incredible image.

He scrambled out of his seat to open her door. She walked right up to the driver's door and then did that double-take of soldiers who only drove American military vehicles when overseas.

Barely able to restrain himself from wrapping an arm around her waist, he led her to the left-hand passenger door and held it open for her.

"What?" she stopped with the door between them. "No greeting of hello, yet jumping to open my door, even if I don't know which is which. What's going on, Pete?"

He didn't know. They were standing on a U.S. military base. And while she perhaps wasn't the most physically beautiful woman he'd ever known, she was close. However, Danielle stopped him cold like no other woman ever had. Her looks combined with the way she carried herself were sufficient to make grunts stop and stare when she was walking across base, even if hers wasn't the face-slap beauty of someone like Sophia Gracie. To his eyes, all others dimmed in comparison to the woman standing a single car-door thickness away.

"Climb on in."

"Not until you explain that look on your face."

"I don't have a mirror, how am I supposed to know what I look like?"

"You look beautiful."

Men weren't supposed to look beautiful, but in Danielle's whispery French accent it was very hard to complain.

"Also like a rascal."

Pete rubbed at his jaw in order to stop himself from reaching out and doing something wholly inappropriate while standing on a military base. He'd save inappropriate for as soon as he could get her alone.

She did that eyebrow-arch-question thing.

He placed a hand on top of her head and pushed down until she gave in with a smile and sat in her seat. He closed the door and circled back around the car.

What was it about this woman?

Enjoy and depart…

Good times…

No attachments…

None of the tools he'd used up until now to manage relationships fit Danielle Delacroix.

This is so stupid, he told himself as they drove out through the security gate.

Why's that?

Pete ignored his own question—resisting the desire to pound his head against the steering wheel—turned north across the Hiji River, and drove through the Toguchi District. In minutes they transitioned from two and three-story concrete buildings crowded hard against the road's edge out into the neat Japanese farmland.

The woman was so goddamn attractive, he didn't even dare look at her for fear of crashing the car. It had been a while since he'd been in a right-hand drive country himself and Japanese roads were painfully narrow with deep concrete drainage ditches close beside them.

# # #

Danielle stared hard out the passenger left-side window. The Japanese countryside was so orderly that even the trees looked like they belonged in a museum. They lined up in perfect rows of impossibly uniform size, ten meters high and one hand wide; they looked phony, like a child's drawing of a forest made with a ruler.

The farms were out of some textbook. She recognized potatoes growing in rows so perfect that they must be hand tended. Why potatoes here? It seemed so mundane. But she couldn't ask.

The bastard hadn't greeted her. Hadn't told her that he was glad to see her. She hadn't been expecting him to take her against the side of the car in broad daylight, but she'd expected *something*. Instead, he'd shoved her down and into the car as if he wanted to hide her from view.

Then he'd muttered to himself.

Stupid? He thought that being with her was stupid? Taking the risk because of their need for each other *was* stupid from a military point of view. But she had been so looking forward to getting away with Pete. She'd said yes before he'd even had a chance to finish asking.

Then he'd called it stupid and refused to explain when she asked why. Was that how he thought of this? Of her? A risk for sex that wasn't really worth it?

Is that all he thought this was? *Sex?*

Sure they'd had sex on the scratchy grass in the NTTR. But they had also made love in the back of the Chinook. There was nothing else to call it. She'd already been gone on him by that point. Now she was pretty sure she was in love with Pete Napier… and he was worried about the trade-off of risk versus sex?

She could feel the ache in her fingers from clenching the door handle. Pete reached the coast road and continued north, still not looking over at her. Why would he? He was ashamed of his need for her and wanted to hide it away. Apparently she was just a fuck buddy, and that wasn't what she'd signed up for. It wasn't what her heart had signed up for.

The view of the Sea of Japan sparkling beneath the morning sun wasn't the only reason her vision had gone watery.

By all the saints, she was a Québécois. A woman of SOAR and she goddamn deserved to be treated like one.

Danielle was gonna kill the man if she sat here a second longer.

"Let's go back."

"Huh, what? Don't be silly." And the bastard kept driving.

"Stop the car."

"Why?"

"Stop the goddamn car, Napier! Or I'll fucking jump!" her shout was so loud inside the car that it hurt her own ears. She didn't look over, but she could feel his shock.

He eased the car onto the narrow shoulder.

She was out the door and moving before the Toyota had fully stopped. She tucked her knapsack over one shoulder, aimed herself back toward base, and started walking. The pavement was rough-surfaced but in good condition.

And she could hear Pete coming up beside her.

Danielle took an abrupt right turn onto the narrow-sand beach, moments before he reached her.

He cursed and called her name.

She kept moving.

He grabbed her arm.

She whirled and gut-punched him hard enough to drop him to the sand.

Danielle turned to keep walking.

An iron-strong hand clamped around her ankle which sent her tumbling down as well. She should have simply rolled with it and come up onto her feet ready to turn and fight.

But her one arm was caught in her knapsack. And Pete didn't let go.

She face planted.

Sand was hard when you hit it with your face. It was all down the front of her blouse and bra in an instant. She rolled over to kick Pete's grip free and could feel the back of her pants scoop several handfuls of grit down her backside.

She shook her leg and he let go.

"What the hell's your problem, Napier?"

"What's yours, Delacroix?" His expression was bewildered as he rubbed at his solar plexus.

"You really don't get it?" Danielle didn't know whether to be angry or simply give up. Rubbing at her face to get the fine sand clear, she pulled up her legs so that her ankles were out of his reach.

"Wouldn't ask if I did."

" *'This is so stupid'?*" She did a fair mimic of his American farm-boy accent.

"I," he squinted at her then looked around to retrieve his sunglasses that had fallen to the beach when she'd leveled him.

Hers had somehow stayed on her face.

"I thought I was speaking to myself."

"Out loud, Napier."

"Didn't mean to."

"You called what we were going to do 'stupid.'"

"Were? Past tense?" Pete's voice was suddenly sad, like a little boy who had just lost his ice cream.

"Could someone please explain men to me?" she asked the world at large. Which consisted of a green Toyota, several hundred meters of beach, and a horizon's worth of ocean shining beneath a blue sky.

"Don't look at me," he held up his hands in surrender.

She rested her forehead on her knees and began cursing.

# # #

Pete recognized most of the French swear words. Though what *tabarnak* (like a church's tabernacle?) had to do with her present mood, he didn't know. Then Danielle went sideways into Italian followed by something that might have been Spanish mixed with…he didn't know what, but she sounded pretty frustrated.

He reached out to brush a comforting hand down her calf, but felt a sharp twinge in his solar plexus and backed off. Damn but she had a good punch.

Her cursing eased off but she still didn't raise her head.

Stupid? This was eight kinds of stupid. He knew so much about Danielle and not just the way she flew and the way she served her country, both of which were so incredible that those alone blinded him.

The one taste he'd had of her back after that first flight had built a whole idiotic world of fantasies about the woman—a set of fantasies that she had totally shattered in the hangar at the NTTR by proving how lame his imagination was when compared to reality.

During their last month of flying together, training together, eating together—and *not* sleeping together—he'd also come to learn about the gentle, thoughtful woman who had crawled up out of a hell he couldn't imagine. A father long gone. A woman who couldn't be bothered to put down the bottle for the sake of her kid. Growing up in a desperate poverty he couldn't imagine, to somehow turn into—

He didn't know what.

No woman had ever so occupied his thoughts, not even Lucy—and he'd married her.

Married her, but never said the L-word except for during "…love, honor, and obey." He'd thought that "honor" was the key word of that ceremony. Which he'd done. She hadn't cared a moment about breaking all three. There was his Hell Hound Cerberus. Betrayal, thy name is…

Not Danielle.

Her curses had softened and ultimately lapsed into silence. She sat on the sand with arms wrapped across shins, forehead on pulled-up knees. He reached out to brush a hand over her head; barely a twinge this time.

"Don't!" she said before he completed the gesture, even though she didn't raise her head.

"What the hell, Delacroix?" at a complete loss he finally dug up a fistful of sand and began pouring it back and forth between his palms.

"How about a sentence longer than four words? And see if you can do it without insulting me in the process."

What in the world was he supposed to do with that? The silence stretched long enough for him to become aware of the black-tailed seagulls. He'd never gotten used to their calls,

Colorado didn't have a whole lot of gulls. Here they were revered, the messengers from the goddess of the fishery. They circled and called lazily overhead as if he wasn't sitting here on the cool sand sinking ever deeper into trouble he didn't understand.

"Try," Danielle prompted him, "explaining why you're with me if you think it's a stupid risk."

A *what?* "It's not a stupid risk."

"Five words. Wow, Napier, really stretching yourself."

"What's nuts, Danielle Delacroix, is how much I want you."

"You're still talking sex."

"No!" Now he was the one shouting. At his soft, "Goddamn it," she finally looked back up at him. He wished she wasn't wearing sunglasses. Her eyes were so expressive and…

"Then what is stupid, Major, if not risking both our careers for sex?"

Speak. In longer sentences? Fine.

"If it was just sex, Danielle, I'd never take the risk. Hell, I can get sex anywhere. Japanese woman can be splendidly compliant and willing if they're in the right mood to—" She didn't need to remove her sunglasses for him to see he was screwing up.

Oh.

"If that's what you thought I was saying, I can see why you got pissed."

Try again.

"See, I've built all of these defenses against women."

"A lot of them?" Was that the hint of a smile?

"Tons. My whole life I've looked for women who could easily come second to my career."

"And what did you find?"

"I found crap!" Which now that he'd said it he knew to be true, perhaps one of the greatest truths he'd ever spoken. "I might as well have spent my time masturbating for all the involvement I felt with most of these women. They were fun, but—" But he needed to leave that subject immediately. "And then you stand there, a drop-dead gorgeous pilot who can quote Greek tragedies,

Batman comics, and flies better than any Chinook pilot I've ever served with."

She was still now. When he needed to read her the most, he couldn't get a clue.

"I want you, Danielle Spiderwoman Delacroix. Like I've never wanted a woman before. To make love to, sure; something you're crazy good at. To fly with, absolutely; something you're even better at than making love, if that's even possible. But there's more there. I don't have the words for it, but when you're not beside me, even for a couple hours, it's like my world stops making sense somehow and I…" his words ran out long before he reached the point he didn't even know how to find, never mind express.

Danielle rolled forward onto her knees until she knelt before him. Leaning in, her face so close that he couldn't look at her sunglass' reflections of both of his own eyes at once, she hesitated one moment.

"I think you said it just fine, Pete." Then she kissed him.

It might be a risk, but he really hadn't liked how it felt when she'd walked away from him, so he wrapped his arms around her and leaned back until she had no choice but to sprawl forward on top of him. He kept her in the kiss as she lay there and hoped to god he would find some way not to screw this up.

Chapter 12

D*anielle contemplated Pete's back* while he sprawled facedown on the mattress beside her. The mattress was thin and lying on a polished wooden floor, but surprisingly comfortable. Even in his sleep, Pete's muscles were clearly defined across his back. His strength inherent in who he was.

He'd taken them to a little Japanese inn with rooms perched out on the edge of a cliff over the sea. It was all very native and she didn't understand a single word or tradition. She'd flown hundreds of sorties during her deployments in war-torn south-west Asia, but East Asia might as well be Neptune for what she knew about it. Well, not a *whole* other planet, so maybe Pluto.

First off he had led her to an *onsen,* a hot-spring fed common bathing room.

"Don't worry, men and women are separated," Pete had whispered into her ear before disappearing through another door without any further instructions.

Maybe it was some cheap payback for refusing to actually have sex on the roadside beach while her underwear was full of sand, or perhaps he thought jumping into the unknown was fun.

Which it was, usually.

At the moment she was still too busy trying to deal with Pete's wandering attempt to pin down his feelings. He not only wanted her, he missed her when they weren't together. No one had ever really missed Danielle Delacroix before—at least not that managed to say it. Or show it. Not anyone…until Pete.

In the *onsen,* Danielle had tried to watch the other women out of the corner of her eye and still had to be prompted in friendly tones that she didn't understand a word of.

Strip off everything and place it in an open cubby hole.

No lockers, no keys to carry with.

She was embarrassed at how much sand had still remained in her clothes, but it was such a relief to no longer have it sandpapering her skin that she got over that quickly. The motor pool car would not be recovering so easily.

Removing her dog tags brought her to a stop. It was stupid, but standing among a half dozen strangers who were all Japanese, six or more inches shorter than she was, and uncaring of their nakedness, it was the tags that were the hardest article of clothing to remove. The hardest to trust that they'd still be tucked away in the cubby when she came back.

A woman—perhaps five feet tall, before she'd been bent nearly double with age and osteoporosis and old enough to be her great-*grand-mère*—finally commanded her to remove them with an upward flick of her hands. Then she'd placed them atop Danielle's clothes and gave her a sharp shove toward the next door. The old woman was surprisingly strong.

Following her guidance, Danielle dipped a wooden bucket into a large pool of scalding water, and moved to sit on an ankle-high stool facing the matron. A pair of brusque and muscular women dressed in white that might have been nurses uniforms moved up behind each of them and began slathering them with a soft-bristle soapy brush.

The old woman chatted away with the other women there. Danielle was clearly the subject, but being taken under the woman's wing—the oldest one in the group by far—apparently opened a path for her easy acceptance.

The elder made a face at Danielle, first wide-eyed and open-mouthed, and then suddenly closed up like someone had pinched her face. Danielle was still trying to figure it out when the bath attendant dumped the bucket of scalding water over her head. Mouth open, Danielle was spluttering and coughing out bath water which all of the women seemed to find completely hilarious.

Another bucket followed the first but she managed to not drink any of it this time. Once the suds were all washed down the central floor drain, they moved to the steaming pool. Those already in the water, made room along the underwater bench that circled the perimeter.

The water was so hot that it took her several tries to immerse herself though she noticed the other women slipped easily into the water—not a one of them had a single word of language in common with her. Pete had dragged her far enough away from Kaneda and the other large military installations that such conveniences were gone, so she did the only thing she could do and let herself float in the water.

The stress of her fight…her *misunderstanding* with Pete drained out of her. And of the month's training. And of her doubts of herself as a woman.

It was funny how Pete, by being so alarmingly male, made her feel so female. It wasn't something she cultivated in herself. Out-perform the men was more her personal motto. Be so competent that they can't ignore you and so pure military that you become a brother-in-arms despite the lack of a penis. Pete made her feel both competent and feminine.

At a tap on her shoulder, she opened her eyes.

The old woman was sitting on the edge of the pool with only her feet in the water. She waved Danielle up.

She needed the woman's steadying hand once she managed to make it up onto the edge, her head swimming lightly with the overheating. The conversations were quieter now, easier. She was no longer aware of her own nakedness as being out of the ordinary. A perfect lassitude lay over her like a warm blanket.

And somehow, that immensely foreign object known as Major Pete Napier had also become familiar. More than familiar. Welcome? Cherished.

Though he would still be required to learn French if he wanted to keep her *amour*.

# # #

Pete lay there and let his sleepy mind follow the light tracery of Danielle's fingers over his back and shoulders.

After the *onsen* they'd eaten udon noodles with thin slivers of pork at a foot-high table while wearing thin wrap-around robes. She had taken to chopsticks quickly, at least quickly enough that she wouldn't starve, and he was able to spend much of the meal admiring how the robe's silk hid then revealed shapes without clinging.

Then she'd laid down beside him and, even as he brushed his hand over her lovely form, fallen asleep to the sound of the sea rushing over the rocks below. He liked this little *ryokan*; the inn was tucked away where only locals found it. Their room was perched on a cliff edge above the Sea of Japan, and the privacy felt as if it went on forever. The smells of the salt sea on the warm breeze wandered through the room.

He'd felt like a voyeur watching her sleep. It was their first time in a proper bed together, even if it was the Japanese version of one; a futon on a polished wood floor. Even asleep, there was a vibrancy to her that drew him in. Made him want to…serve and protect?

To lose his brain, more like. But he'd watched her sleep until he'd joined her in dreams.

Now the day had passed and the room was rich with the amber light of sunset against his closed eyelids as her hand slid once more down his spine.

"Danielle?"

"Hmm?" her hum was as soft as the evening breeze.

"Don't ever stop doing that."

"Roll over and I'll do far more than that."

Well, that was an invitation that he wasn't going to turn down. He soon lay on his back and, as promised, her fingers continued their light investigation of his torso.

"One, two," her hand traced over one of his arms. "Three," along his ribs.

"Four," her hand slid over his thigh and he finally knew what she was counting—bullet holes.

"Any more?"

"Right foot. Thought I told you about when my little brother tried to amputate my foot with a shotgun. No? Thankfully, I'd only loaded it with rocksalt until he learned some basic skills. The rest were, uh, in places I probably shouldn't be mentioning."

She leaned in and teased the first bullet wound with a soft scrape of teeth.

"Nope," he refused her.

Danielle continued teasing him, pressing herself against him.

He managed to resist until she slid a hand down past his waist and cupped him ever so gently. He knew it would just stereotype him as male, but there was a feeling of safety and security when she did that. It was perhaps the most erotic thing a woman had ever done to him. It was so complete a sensation that he could form no thought beyond pleasure.

"One," she whispered against the skin of his arm.

"And two," putty in her hands and he didn't care. "Both in Syria. A couple years apart, before and after the start of the Arab Spring." Her security clearance was high enough anyway.

Without releasing her hand from around him, instead starting a gentle massage that made him so hard each pulse of blood almost hurt as it throbbed, she moved her mouth to his ribs.

"Shit! That tickles!"

"The Rapier is ticklish?"

"I'd prefer it if you didn't sound so delighted by the discovery," he tried to squirm aside without breaking her hold on him because damn that felt good.

"Third?" she attacked him again. He tried to find ticklish spots on her, but couldn't seem to land one quickly enough.

"Myanmar," he finally confessed on a gasp. "A week in the hospital and ten more to recover."

"Fourth?" her voice turned into a purr as she nuzzled the inside of his thigh.

"Goddamn dustbowl," nobody got through two years in Iraq clean. The fact that he'd been flying deep into Iran when he was shot and his crew chief killed was just a technicality.

And then it was his turn to inspect her body. Her skin was like liquid gold, a smoothly perfect covering that he'd never had a chance to properly appreciate.

He leaned in to taste the inside of her thigh as she continued to do the same for him.

They shifted closer and closer until they were pleasuring each other and rising together. They crested on the same wave, holding on as the last of the light bled from the windows and the last of the shudders bled from their bodies.

Still they held each other.

It was the most natural of motions when they shifted so that she lay her cheek on his shoulder. And still her gentle fingers held him.

The way the woman made love, there was no questioning where he was meant to be. Now or ever.

Her *Monsieur* Cupid had shot him straight through the heart.

# # #

Having slept through much of the day, they spent the night making love and talking about their pasts, the parts you didn't discuss with anyone less than a lover.

Danielle knew precisely what made Pete moan like a man dying, but hadn't known that about the unavailable woman he had loved in high school. Or the cheerleader who had taken his virginity in the back of his dad's pickup. "Starting raining on us halfway through but there was no way I was stopping that close to gold. Not a whole lot of cuddling afterwards. I made sure our rematch was in a nice, dry hayloft."

His sympathy at her being alone in the world was sincere. And his anger surprising. The story of her abandoning father and alcoholic mother were so ingrained in her psyche that there was little emotion attached anymore. When she laid out the true depths of the situation, Pete had fumed on her behalf as if that would somehow change the past.

And it did, in a way. It showed her what support was like, real support. When someone was so far in your corner that they would fight the battle for you if they could.

For that gift, she had loved him tender.

And shortly before dawn, when they wandered into battle stories of his divorce and the destruction of so many youthful dreams, they had loved hard until it was purged from his soul. They welcomed the daybreak laughing together over the joy of being alive even as the orgasms shattered them.

By the time they were headed back to base, Danielle knew a truth.

She didn't love Pete Napier.

Love was far too simple a word for the depth and breadth of so much feeling. She could spend a lifetime getting to know the man and never have enough.

Though as she relaxed in the car seat and watched the sunrise gild the odd forests and diagrammatically perfect farmland of Japan, she was fairly sure her body had all it could stand at the moment.

But even that thought evoked warm feelings that rippled gently over nerves she'd thought spent. She slid a hand over and tucked her fingertips beneath Pete's thigh as he drove, the connection between them not needing any words as they floated along by the sea.

Well, Spiderwoman had found her own personal Superman and she wouldn't be filing any complaints with the casting department.

Chapter 13

P*ete was tracking the* USS *Germantown.* She was based out of Sasebo, Japan and the six hundred-foot ship was on the move.

Sasebo, Kadena Air Base, and the mouth of the Qiantang River in China made a neat triangle around five hundred miles on a side.

The *Germantown* was an LDS—landing dock ship—capable of deploying multiple helicopters and large hovercraft at a moment's notice. A powerful rapid deployment force. It would appear to any watching Chinese radar that the *Germantown* was on one of her frequent patrols from Japan down to Taiwan.

Tonight her course would bring her atypically close to shore, though she'd still remain outside both the twelve-mile territorial waters and the twenty-four-mile contiguous waters of China. However, she'd be deep inside the exclusive economic zone of two-hundred miles. While this wasn't necessary to make the passage, it was done on occasion to serve as a reminder to China that the U.S. could deploy heavy forces much farther forward than any other nation could hope to match.

The USS *Germantown* had no need to go to Taiwan—a week ago Taiwan hadn't been on her schedule until the following month. And she certainly had no need to pass so close.

Her entire voyage and its relatively close passage to China's shore actually served only one purpose, to distract the Chinese from paying any attention to the *Germantown's* sister ship.

The *Ashland*, also based out of Sasebo, also would be cruising toward Taiwan a hundred miles farther offshore. Rather than carrying their usual complement of Marine helos, she was traveling empty. The *Ashland* would be the base for the 5E's operation.

Five hundred miles from Kadena to Qiantang was much too far for ease of operation. The Chinook and DAP Hawk could operate from five hundred miles out, but the Little Birds couldn't. And lingering on site so close to the Chinese mainland brought on a whole other set of issues.

The Black Hawk and Chinook could stay aloft as long as they could get mid-air refueling every four hours and the crew could stay conscious. But the Little Birds *LeeLoo* and *Linda* were limited to two hours and three hundred miles per sortie and then they had to land somewhere to refuel. Thankfully, the position of the *Ashland* placed China well within the tiny gunships' range.

By placing the *Ashland* a hundred and twenty miles offshore, they could fly the night's mission from there. A hundred and twenty miles, two-fifty round trip, well that was a sweet spot.

Pete ordered everyone aloft at full dusk. They slipped out of Kadena Air Base with no one the wiser. Two hours later all four helos landed on the deck of the *Ashland*. Pete had always liked these ships.

Unlike the big aircraft carriers, or even the massive helicopter-carrying LHDs, the Navy crew to run the *Ashland* was relatively small. With the standard complement of a couple hundred Marines and all of their craft left ashore, this should be a very quiet operation.

Pete had considered leaving the Little Birds behind; this op really only required the Chinook and the DAP could offer plenty of protection.

"Don't be a *Newfie!*"

Pete decided it was better to not ask for a translation of this one in case Danielle calling him a Newfoundlander was even more disparaging than it sounded. She'd proceeded to talk him out of leaving *Linda* and *LeeLoo* behind by listing her reasons.

"One, if anything goes south in this operation, you absolutely want their power close behind us. If the Black Hawk were damaged or lost, my Chinook would be very vulnerable. The *Carrie-Anne* is an assault craft, not an attack craft. Two…"

Pete didn't know why he'd ever tried to argue with Danielle, every single time he'd tried in the last month, he'd lost.

"…leaving half the team behind for our first-ever mission. *C'est vraiment poche pour le morale.*" At his uncertain expression she translated, "it would suck for morale and you really need to learn French, though that's Québécois. Literally it's *truly pocket* and I couldn't tell you why we say it that way."

Granted, though. It would suck to be left behind.

"Three…"

She never stopped simply because she'd already won—which never failed to make him smile.

"We should have the whole team along because of the unexpected."

Pete had to admit, he did like the layers of backup it provided. He'd always preferred to keep a mission as lean as he could. And if they'd done that at bin Laden's compound, they'd have been screwed. When they lost a helo at landing, the tiers of backup they already had in place made it cost them less than two minutes. Aside from the forty million dollars when they had to blow up the crashed helo.

So, the full flight of the 5E landed on the aft deck of the *Ashland,* taking up all of the available space.

The deck service crew was hand-picked and as lean as possible, but still they kept gawking at the birds as they attached temporary tie-downs. The grapes—purple-vested deck crew who ran out refueling lines to all of the craft—kept tripping over themselves in the desire to look the craft over despite the dimmed nighttime-op deck lights.

"Last chance to swim back to shore!" Danielle called out over the radio. That earned a laugh. In minutes everyone was out on deck, stretching, shaking out limbs, doing some light calisthenics even though the flight to the ship hadn't been all that long. The rest of the night would be.

Danielle headed over to LCDR Luke Altman, and Pete let himself drift along to the rear ramp of the Chinook in her wake. The SEAL team members weren't doing any workouts, they were going over their gear once more. That's when he figured something out. SEALs were always careful, but these guys were...

"Hey Luke, I thought you were on Team 5. When did you go DEVGRU?" Which most civilians thought was still named SEAL Team Six, not true for about thirty years.

None of the SEALs reacted except Luke who rose very slowly to his feet.

"What makes you say that, Pete?"

Pete had forgotten quite how big a man Altman was.

"You just made his argument for him, Commander Altman," Danielle spoke as if there wasn't a very pissed looking SEAL suddenly looming over them, his face lit red and dangerous by the ship's night-operations deck lights.

"Your guys aren't moving like I'm used to your guys moving," Pete explained keeping his voice as casual as Danielle's in hopes that Luke didn't decide to break them in two over his knee and toss them overboard. "Team 5 dudes would be kicking back, maybe taking a quick nap."

"We are invading China tonight."

"Only a little," Danielle argued. "If you really want to invade China—"

She wasn't about to reveal that he'd just been in Tibet, was she? He could get his ass fried for—

"—there's this rare blue flower I need. It's at the base of a Tibetan mountain that leads you to a monastery high on the cliffs. And—"

Pete and Luke laughed together. Luke in chagrin and Pete in relief. Doubting Danielle's discretion was a pointless exercise. It was always perfect, just like her lists of reasoned arguments. Yet by the same unfathomable logic, her judgment included being with him. Danielle had said this wasn't just sex between them, and he'd agreed. But what had he agreed to? In her superior brand of perception was he…"The One" for her?

He swallowed hard.

Pete trusted her implicitly, but had she suddenly gone blind? He was a bad bet for a woman like her. Bad bet? A dead loss, more like. He had a proven track record, bad.

"Tell me again," Danielle was thankfully focused on Luke, "why you aren't going in with a diver vehicle?"

"I would have preferred that, but the Chinese coast is wired underwater within an inch of its life. They have more microphones down there than we sunk outside of Russia's harbors back in the fifties and sixties."

"So, they're more vulnerable up on the surface."

Luke nodded, "You'll dump us as deep in the harbor as you can. We take this Zodiac," he hooked a thumb toward the rubber boat they'd loaded in the back of her Chinook, "and sneak in the rest of the way. Same trick in reverse coming back out."

"If everything goes well," Pete put in.

"Chances of which are…?" Danielle had on that smile she'd shown the moment before attacking him back at the *ryokan*.

Luke apparently didn't know how to read that yet, but he'd learn. The DEVGRU commander shrugged.

Danielle laughed and wandered back to follow her crew chiefs' inspection of the bird. No one redid the preflight on a bird after such a simple flight, but Danielle and her crew did.

He glanced around and saw that every member of the 5E was doing it to their craft as well. Just like DEVGRU. The woman was never going to stop surprising him.

"Got it bad, Pete," Luke spoke softly beside him.

"Yeah, I do."

So "bad" that he hadn't even caught onto what Luke was saying until after the Lieutenant Commander turned back and returned to his own team.

# # #

"Sophia, talk to me."

Danielle was flying in the lead. Pete had arrayed the three weaponized birds behind her, the two Little Birds in close, and the big hammer of *Beatrix* the DAP Hawk trailing a half-mile behind so that Rafe could provide the unexpected response to any rude surprises.

"*Olá,* my friend Danielle. It is so good to hear from you."

Danielle opened her mouth to remind Sophia that this was a mission, not a friendly chat over a meal. But before she had a chance…

"Our friends are very, how you say…grouchy tonight. Many boats have left the harbor of Hangzhou at the mouth of the Qiantang to move out beside the *Germantown.* Kadena Air Force Command, unaware of our operation, has moved four F-18 jets into a loose formation a dozen miles seaward of the *Germantown.* This I think is a good addition to our distraction. All of the noise they are making is now south of your position and continuing down the coast. Security forces in the harbor are down at least thirty percent."

As she'd been speaking, Danielle could see that Sophia was feeding tactical displays to Pete, but she didn't have time to look at it. Her mind had the bandwidth, barely, but her eyes didn't.

Flying just a dozen feet above the East China Sea at close to two hundred miles an hour took a great deal of concentration.

At this speed, rogue waves would slap her out of the sky faster than she could sneeze. A small fishing boat could radio in a warning to the Chinese Coast Guard just as fast as a patrol craft, so she had to avoid every single boat.

It was like racing a slalom course. Turn one, shipping lane patrol vessel. Turn two, fishing boat with outriggers and bright lights to draw the fish to the surface. Through the center of a gate defined by an oil supertanker and a coastal ferry.

She could feel herself freezing up, a little too tight on the controls, not as smooth as she should be. Not rising the extra two feet on a turn to make sure she didn't bury a rotor tip in the waves.

What would Spidey do?

He'd loosen up and swing with it. Let the dark night slide by as he slalomed between various craft and the mapped listening buoys.

She found a smoother rhythm, found the groove as she rolled toward shore. It was…Pete. Not the rhythm of their lovemaking, he always made that gloriously unexpected. No, it was the rhythm of his sleeping breath, perfectly matched to the easy step and shift of the powerful *Carrie-Anne*.

Once she smoothed out, the mission clock finally started moving again. It had been creeping the whole first half of the flight from the *Ashland* toward their target. Now that she was in the flow it was moving apace.

At the outer barrier islands she called, "Ready alert," to the SEALs.

She swirled around the outermost islands, small outcroppings of steep rock.

That crossed them from the open ocean into the thirty-mile wide outer harbor, so she called, "Three minutes." She could take them another ten miles. Maybe a little more.

She made it four minutes and thirteen miles when everything started happening at once and she called twenty seconds. This was her safe limit even in a stealth craft.

The lights of Hangzhou Harbor and Shanghai city came over the horizon. They had been a distant glow, but she'd remained so close to the water that they remained invisible until she was just five miles out from the rocky mainland. The city was set back several more miles from the wide open harbor.

Less than eight miles to the Jiangnan Shipyards. She could see the tops of the tall construction cranes, though the ships under construction were still below the horizon.

The ramp light went on as Jason the rear gunner began lowering the back gate.

"Surface craft north and south, three miles distant," Sophia reported.

Danielle's altitude was now two feet, which placed her pilot's seat at eight. That would have been high enough to see the other boats, but Danielle had turned sideways and slid the body of the Chinook down between two wave peaks. By continuing sideways at twenty-five miles an hour, she managed to stay between the waves with the bulk of the helo in the trough. The rolling swells ranged around ten feet high, so they hid half of the *Carrie-Anne*. A passing boat would see only the top half of the helo and the big twin rotors…

Except it was ten at night and her helicopter was painted pitch black.

"Slick," was Luke's compliment which she was too busy to process until after he said, "We're gone," and his voice disappeared from the intercom.

"Clear," Jason reported less than five seconds later and the hydraulics kicked in to close the ramp.

Danielle raised the *Carrie-Anne* just enough to get the Chinook's belly clear of the waves and aimed back toward the *Ashland*.

# # #

Pete knew he was a damn good pilot, but he'd never seen anyone do that with a Chinook before.

He wanted to put a hand to his chest and try pumping some air into his oxygen-starved lungs; he'd been holding his breath without realizing it while Danielle had settled them down between the wave crests.

But he didn't want to miss a single nuance on their interconnected controls to understand how smoothly she'd done it. No wonder she made love the way she did. She must integrate her entire nervous system into everything she did. Her control was so perfect he could just as easily imagine the Chinook was moving her as the other way around.

She stayed breathtakingly low all of the way back to the *Ashland* sliding easily around the obstacles that Sophia identified from her Avenger flying on high. Danielle didn't rise above ten feet until she reached the ship and had to climb to reach the deck.

An hour and a hundred-and-fifty miles each way and she hadn't done a single thing he could correct.

And if she was going to choose him, he would give up his normal state of idiocy and stop arguing with her.

Chapter 14

*P*arked back on the deck of the USS *Ashland* a hundred miles offshore China and doing nothing worked for Pete—for under ten minutes.

Sophia had the Avenger aloft to keep an eye on Hangzhou Harbor. The problem was that she and her copilot were flying the RPA in the white control box back at Kadena Air Base. Which made it impossible to just "drop in" and look over her shoulder.

Aboard the *Ashland,* Pete bulled his way into the Plot Room—perhaps the most secure room on any ship—partly by nudging Danielle in front of him every time they met male resistance. At first she wasn't happy with his manipulations, but eventually—if he read her correctly and he hoped he did—she was amused by how well it worked on the swabbies. After all, what chance did they stand against the power of a female Night Stalker.

The Avenger, which Sofia had named *Raven* for being an RPA bird—finally one that wasn't one of Danielle's female heroines—could stay aloft for twenty hours on a load of fuel.

The side aperture radar offered a surprisingly clear view the distant harbor and the shipyards from sixty thousand feet and a hundred miles offshore.

"Yes," Sophia reported when they were on the right frequency, "I tracked the SEALs successfully to their destination." She rolled back the video feed that she was supplying to the ship as she talked. In moments he was again watching the *Carrie-Anne* sliding along between the boats and the outer harbor islands.

The ship's captain whistled, "Now that's some pretty flying. Nice, Major."

"Thanks, but the Captain was pilot-in-command."

"Which Captain?"

Pete pointed at Danielle standing close beside him. They were all crowded close to look at the big LCD screen showing the RPA's feed. He was thankful for the chance to rub shoulders with her in public.

"In that case, that's *real* nice, Captain." The smile he sent her didn't even worry Pete any more. Danielle might have stood a little straighter, but otherwise didn't react. Had Pete sounded so sexist in the past? Probably. Being around women like the ones in the 5E forced a man to reevaluate.

"There," Sophia's voice drew all attention back to the screen. The helicopter twisted, then kept flying sideways with the waves, though there was no way to see on the display why she'd done that.

Moments later, a blip appeared off the stern of the Chinook, and then disappeared.

"If I do not know where the plan is they go, I would not be able to follow them." Sophia used a light pen to mark their track on the screen; the blip on the image reappearing only occasionally to mark the track the SEALs were taking.

"Here, they make contact with the Chinese Coast Guard super-ship."

Jiangnan Shipyard was a maze of construction. A half-dozen vessels ranging from two to eight hundred feet were up in dry docks. As many more floated beside long piers where supplies and machinery were cluttered thickly together. The scattered tracking they had on the SEAL team completely disappeared in the snarl.

"Time of last contact?"

"2215 hours," Sophia announced.

Both Pete and Danielle immediately adjusted the dials on their wrist watches. "That was forty-five minutes ago."

"Nothing since."

Pete glanced at Danielle and she grimaced.

"He said it would take a minimum of four hours."

"Shit! What the hell are we supposed to do for four hours?" Actually he had some ideas on that, but he wasn't dumb enough to suggest it.

# # #

Danielle knew the mission plan well enough that she could follow every move, at least every move that the SEAL team wasn't having to make up as they went.

At 2215, Luke and the other three SEALs had arrived at the Jiangnan Shipyard.

Next they'd find their way past the outer breakwater to stow their rubber boat under a dock.

By 2245 the SEALs would scale the ocean side of an eight-hundred foot long Coast Guard cutter, because the dock side was sure to be guarded. The ship was still under construction so there should be multiple points of entry, they were counting on that.

Inside the ship by 2300 and racing the clock and the Chinese security guards.

She and Pete met up with the rest of the 5E crew at 2400 hours for lunch in the ship's mess.

None of them ate very well.

At 0030, the Night Stalkers attempted to start up a Frisbee game between the helicopters crowded together on the aft deck. There was barely room for the four birds. The stars were lost behind a light overcast and the deck was pitch black except for subtle perimeter lights that warned you of a forty-foot plunge from deck to ocean about five steps before you took it. When they almost lost The Whistler disc over the side, they'd given up on that.

By now the SEALs should have infiltrated the command area of the superstructure. They'd be recording every aspect of the ship from the placement of the heavy deck guns to the best paths for future boarding if they ever had to attack one of these ships. The Activity's intel geeks had gone after the construction plans, with surprisingly little luck. They must be stored on a server that wasn't connected to anything else.

Recording the ship's layout was the *secondary* mission.

Now at 0100, if they were anywhere close to on schedule, they should be entering the Chinese equivalent of the *Ashland's* Plot Room. Modern ships were less about the amount of steel in their hull and more about the computer and control systems being used aboard them. A system had to be able to analyze a target that was still two hundred miles over the horizon as being friendly or hostile. Then they must decide to fire on it before they in turn could actually launch a missile—many of the modern missiles had a hundred-mile range and if the enemy craft was supersonic, safety margins went away far too quickly.

The SEAL team had two *primary* missions—a piece of classic military doublespeak for "don't screw up either one." First find out exactly what electronics were installed on the ship, and second put in an undetectable tap. The goal was to transmit every electronic command to the U.S. intelligence agencies, using China's own equipment and antennas. It would be a variable-frequency, high-density squirt transmission, almost impossible to trace. That's if they even noticed it in the first place.

By 0130 Danielle was eyeing dark corners to drag Pete into for mindless sex. It wasn't that she wanted sex; it was about the farthest thing from her interest at the moment. She simply needed to be doing something. The rocking of the big ship on the relatively quiet ocean wouldn't normally be enough to bother her, but in the near pitch darkness, she always seemed on the verge of catching a boot when she encountered an unexpected angle to the deck.

At 0200 she went looking for him and found him in the middle of the aft deck, arms crossed and glaring at the Chinook. Within moments the entire crew was there, as if they'd all homed in together at the same moment.

A buzz of, "This is killing me." "Still no word." "What if—" "How soon—" swarmed to life.

"We go now," Danielle's flat statement silenced the whole group. Because they were sure as hell achieving nothing out here in the emptiness of the East China Sea.

"We don't know when they'll need us."

"It's two in the morning. If they don't need us before six a.m., the sun will be up and we'll have to wait until tomorrow night."

Groans rippled around the group.

# # #

"What are you suggesting?" Pete's voice silenced them. He had some ideas of his own.

Knowing Danielle, it was probably the same idea, so he answered his own question. "The *Carrie-Anne* and the *Beatrix* are aloft in five minutes."

Danielle's nod confirmed her thoughts.

"We have four hours of fuel. If they need us, we'll be that much closer."

"*We* don't!" Dozer protested. "My Little Bird only carries two hours. Even if I throw Patty overboard, it's not going to help enough."

"Hey!" Patty protested, but was ignored. So she smacked Dozer on the back of the head and he grinned at her.

"The Little Birds will follow either when we get the call from the insertion team or at 0400, two hours to sunrise."

None of the Little Bird pilots looked pleased, but it was the best solution Pete had. If they flew the two main birds a hundred miles closer to the coast and circled, they'd be able to respond to a call in ten minutes instead of forty-five. The increased risk of being spotted the longer they were there was marginal, as long as they were careful.

As they prepared the birds for flight, he and Danielle were alone for just a moment.

"I've got a bad feeling about this, Spiderwoman. Like we're already too late."

She nodded, her eyes wide enough to catch the dim red deck lights.

"Let's get up in the air, then you hustle your pretty ass to the China coast. You hustle it hard."

"Roger that."

Chapter 15

*D*anielle hustled her ass hard.

They were aloft in under five minutes. This time the DAP Hawk was tight on her blind spot; she felt exposed, uncomfortable without the familiar Little Birds also close by. The ADAS camera offered a full three-hundred-and-sixty-degree view, but the back left quadrant was always a weak spot for any rotorcraft pilot. Rafe tucked the *Beatrix* in there nice and tight which made her feel a little better.

Sophia was calling out the locations of marine and air traffic before Danielle was a mile off the deck of the *Ashland*.

For the first half of the flight no one spoke, and Danielle flew on raw nerves. Unable to stand it any longer, she flicked the intercom control to pilots only.

"Talk to me, Pete."

"Sure, you need me to take over?"

"For a minute, sure."

"I have command," his hands were smooth and confident on the controls.

She removed her hands and flexed them, tried shaking out the nerves that rippled along them. Within thirty seconds, she couldn't stand it any more and took up the collective and cyclic once more.

"I have command," she called.

"Well, that was a long break."

"Best I've got."

"Hell, Spidey, worst you've got is better than most folks' best."

"Worst I got? I catch a blade and we all go for a swim unless the Chinese Coast Guard feels like rescuing us."

"I wouldn't worry about it," Pete's voice didn't sound forced in its cheerfulness. Since when had The Rapier become cheerful?

"Why not?"

"Oh, you catch a blade this close to the Never Exceed Speed then we'll all be dead in seconds. After that we'll sink like a stone. In the big picture of possibilities, I wouldn't worry about the Chinese if we crash."

"Since when did you turn so chipper? What have you done with my dark, broody lover?" Danielle swung around an ore carrier inbound from Australia. Sophia, watching from far above, sent her scooting south to avoid the next boat.

"Dark and broody? Me?"

"*Oui!*"

"It was when you said *tu et moi*. A beautiful woman, a hot pilot, and a sexy French accent. Somewhere along the way I decided I was a pretty damned lucky guy. That brightened up my day quite a bit."

"Okay, my handsome hunk of a lover. Guess what?"

"What?"

"We're flying into China. And if we're caught, we'll probably start a war. Definitely tossed in a shitty Chinese jail for spying or treason or something."

"Could be a problem. Unless their cells are co-ed. You, me, a hard bunk. Possibilities."

"Men!" Danielle gave it her best scoff. He might have sex on the brain, but he was making her feel better despite that.

They arrived as close as she dared to the outer harbor barrier islands and turned to circle back out to sea in a holding pattern when the radio crackled to life.

Danielle was glad for Pete's steady hands still riding the controls or she might have actually delivered them into the watery depths outside of Hangzhou Harbor.

# # #

"Pete. Tell me you were smart," were the first words over the Chinook's radio.

Pete didn't need to recognize Luke's voice, he was the only one who should be on this frequency. Before answering, Pete flipped the intercom back to include the three crew chiefs in the rear of the helo. They didn't need to hear about his relationship with Danielle, but they deserved to know exactly what they were flying into.

"Me or Danielle, can't be sure; we're both pretty damn smart you know. Currently at the outer island of Zhoushan to the south edge of the harbor."

"Good! You're here. That's a relief. We're boxed in. Every goddamn ship that went chasing down the coast after the *Germantown* has come back. There's no way we can move back out to sea."

"Your alternative is for us to fly into a crowded harbor?"

"We've spent the last hour dancing with security forces back and forth across this goddamn cutter. They aren't sure that we're here but they will be pretty damn fast. We got it done, so we need to get out before they get too suspicious."

"Roger, hang on."

Danielle had been circling them slowly off the south entrance to the wide outer harbor. The SEALs were deep in a secure military shipyard along the north shore—nine minutes away— across thirty miles of waters thick with pissed off Chinese Navy and Coast Guard vessels just looking for a fight to assuage their egos after the *Germantown* decoy had blithely ignored them during its passage.

Pete racked his brain for everything he'd read about Hangzhou Harbor and the Qiantang River. Heavy population to the north, very few people to the south where usable land was limited quickly by jagged rocky heights.

North of the SEAL team's current location was even worse. Over the ridge from Hangzhou sprawled the megalopolis of Shanghai.

Coal, ore, and lots of oil shipping would also be clogging both harbors, far more imports than even the U.S. needed. China was sucking mud. Their economy was in screaming growth. They had the labor pool to support it, but not the developed resources. They were switching from being a top global exporter to becoming one of its top importers.

Which didn't help him at all.

It was a city of incredible tourist attractions that he'd always wanted to see.

Two World Heritage Sites; one on a lake and the other inland. West Lake had one of the archetypal gardens that had influenced the rest of China and Japan for over a thousand years. The city had the oldest Catholic church and the oldest mosque in China… which didn't do the trapped SEALs any damn good at all.

The streets of Shanghai were…useless.

The—

"What time is it?"

"0310," Danielle responded.

"What's the date?"

"September—"

"No, the Chinese date."

"How am I supposed to know that?"

"Come on, Spidey. Thought you knew everything." Pete should not be enjoying himself at the moment, but he really was. The adrenaline was buzzing hot through his veins. If he was right, this was going to totally kick ass. And he was going to have the hottest Chinook pilot in the military to give them a chance of pulling this off. And if he screwed up, they'd all be dead so it wouldn't matter anyway.

"Sophia," Pete clicked onto the Avenger's frequency which would relay his call back to her container in Japan. "What's today's date on the Chinese calendar?"

There was a long pause as she accessed the Internet.

"Eighth lunar month. Eighteen day."

"Perfect! The tide in Hangzhou. What time does it come in?"

Another long pause.

"0350 and—"

He didn't care about the afternoon tide. He flipped back to Luke's frequency.

"Hey, Altman, buddy. I need you to check something out for me."

"What? Make it quick."

"I need you and your team to take your little boat for a scenic cruise northwest, I repeat northwest from your current position."

"Inland? Up the fucking Qiantang River?" There was a very satisfying choking sound in Altman's throat. Unnerving a DEVGRU Commander was even more fun than he'd thought.

"You must be mid-channel under the Jiubao Highway Bridge in exactly twenty-seven minutes. Believe me when I say there won't be any other boats there."

"Shit! Twenty-seven?" Pete could hear scrambling in the background. "What do I do when I get there?"

"Go surfing."

Altman didn't have time for more than a few choice words before he got moving, but they were very satisfying to Pete's ego.

They'd be even more satisfying if they all survived this.

Chapter 16

Danielle listened as Pete called the Little Birds to come rushing in, but they were almost an hour out. They'd be no help in the plan's execution, neither would the DAP Hawk. But, he said, they might need all three to cover their escape.

Why didn't that sound good?

Whatever Pete's plan was, it was going to happen in twenty-six minutes.

Next he directed the DAP Hawk to remain outside the harbor and to be ready for all hell to break loose at 0355, right after whatever magical moment Pete had figured out.

She still didn't have a clue.

"Let's fly southwest."

"Southwest?" Danielle looked up at the mountains of Mainland China on the south side of Hangzhou Harbor. What lay in front of them didn't look the least little bit like water. It looked like farmland backed by rugged mountains. "Have you fucking lost it?"

"Trust me, Spiderwoman. I'm spinning a delicate thread here."

"I'll Spiderwoman you right in the snoot! *Merde!* You are so lucky my hands are busy."

"Trust me, Danielle."

And just that simply, she did. She wasn't sure how she felt about his power over her if *Trust me, Danielle* was all it took. And she really did, apparently with her very life.

She turned southwest and goosed the *Carrie-Anne* to life. There wasn't time to think about her heart.

He guided her ashore between Yuyao and Ningbo, which meant nothing to her, but she could see them marked on the tactical display spread on the inside of her visor. They crossed a pair of highways and then she was in topography she recognized. Ridge and valley. Like the back byways of the Appalachian Mountains, the Chinese mountains were coated by lush growth with streams and rivers in the bottom of every valley.

And like Afghanistan, the valleys were brutally steep and unpredictable in their sharp turns. Her predictive software didn't know what to make of the tiny hamlets and ridge-perching villas.

So it was up to real-time and reflexes, which was actually her favorite kind of flying. She still needed the enhanced electronic view, but she had to solve moment to moment the best line of attack, and the best route.

A narrow twist lead to an abrupt waterfall.

She soared up the face, could practically feel the cool spray that speckled the windshield. Then bursting out among a cluster of riverside homes above the steep falls.

"These people are phoning us in like mad. I can feel it."

"You think they'd expect anyone other than their own military to fly through these valleys? We're probably safer here than out in the harbor. And if they do call us in, radar isn't going to show squat. Definitely not a stealth Chinook sliding through their mountain valleys."

She hadn't thought of it that way.

"0338," Pete called out the time. "C'mon, Sweet Lady. Show me what you can do."

"I'm not sweet!" she managed between gritted teeth.

"Sure you are, Spiderwoman. You're about the sweetest damn woman there ever was. I mean you put up with me, don't you?"

That earned him a snort of laughter from the crew chiefs on the intercom who would be using their miniguns to brace themselves into position and scanning for likely targets.

"Put up with—" it came out as a ragged sputter. She was flying into decidedly hostile territory and he still hadn't told her why or what she'd be doing there.

Pete was deep in communication with Sophia deciding on the best routes, sometimes leaving Danielle on her own, sometimes directing her to cross over into the next valley or start trending north.

If she wasn't putting up with him, then what was she doing?

"0342. Eight minutes to the G15 bridge. We can't be late."

Danielle flipped a control to project the overall tactical display from Sophia's Avenger for a moment. Then she flipped back to the immediate terrain view while her mind analyzed what she'd seen.

0343.

Seven minutes.

"The SEALs are reporting pursuit," Sophia called.

"Let me know when it breaks off," Pete replied calmly.

Man was so goddamn sure of himself. With reason. He was a master tactician who had just led the 5E to the fastest unit certification in history.

Well, if he was going to be so sure of himself, she'd do the same.

The Chinook was too deep in the valleys to talk directly to the SEALs. Radios were either line-of-sight or bounced off satellites, and the Chinook's present flight path sucked for both.

Staying in the deep valleys, she had to keep her speed down if she didn't want to round some corner and fly into a valley's headwall. But if she slowed down at all, she was going to be too late.

"Only Chinese fly in China? Fine."

She tipped the cyclic forward for speed and reefed up on the collective with her left hand to climb.

"Come on, *Carrie-Anne.* You're a leather-clad lady. Fly!"

She cleared the valley wall at 0344 at a hundred and ninety-six miles an hour, the very outer limit of what the Chinook could do.

Once above the ridge line, she stayed high. They'd traveled deep into the mountains south of Hangzhou Harbor to avoid the more populous area. Seventeen miles straight-line flight.

She should be there within thirty seconds of schedule. Danielle kept the nose down.

"Stay on your toes, guys," she called back to the three crew chiefs.

Sophia's data was streaming into Pete's station. He was making adjustments to her course, but there was little he could do now. It was a flat-out race.

"Pursuit is breaking off, Pete," Luke's transmission crackled back to life. "What don't I know?"

"You'll know the signal to move. When you get it, go upriver and go full tilt."

At two minutes out she considered getting Pete on the private intercom for just a moment.

But why should he have all the fun? *Sweetest damn woman* and all that…she left the intercom wide open.

"Petey?" she did her best to make her voice a caress as she crossed over the last ridge south of the Hangzhou and plunged earthward back toward the low farmlands—but now far deeper into China.

"What?" Now Pete's voice was the one that was strained.

"I'm not just putting up with you." She shot over terraced fields, circled wide around the Hangzhou International Airport, and was once again over the water. She was eighty miles farther into China than when she'd left the East China Sea.

"No?" his voice was strained as he called the next order. "Get west of the bridge and be ready to race inland."

"No," she kept her voice smooth and calm as she aimed the *Carrie-Anne* for the middle of the river. It was only a couple hundred yards wide here. The sides were lined with concrete, tiers of concrete. For this channel to fill was going to take one hell of a tide.

Then she saw why they were here at four in the morning and had to swallow hard to keep her voice steady.

"In addition to putting up with you," she slid down low over the water. "I also love you."

There was a *whoop* from one of the crew chiefs.

"But for this," she glanced once more at the nightmare that the cameras were projecting inside her visor. "For this, I'm going to kill you, *Petey!*"

The tide wasn't flowing in, it was *boiling in.* She'd read about the Nova Scotia tidal bore. A wave, often as much as a five feet high, washed up the Bay of Fundy on its way to creating the world's largest tide.

But the Hangzhou tidal bore was a roiling wall of breaking waves two stories high and rising.

"Ramp down!" she called back.

She hopped the Chinook over the Jiubao Bridge just as the tidal bore crashed against its pillars. Spray plumed a dozen stories into the air close behind them.

And then she settled down into the water just ahead of the on-rushing tidal bore.

There was a move called a Delta Queen where a Chinook landed in water, preferably calm water, and allowed itself to sink slightly—just until its cargo bay deck was awash in a foot of water. A racing rubber Zodiac, driven by SEALs with a death wish, could shoot aboard at thirty miles an hour and then the Chinook would take back off. As they climbed, it was always a trick to dump the six or seven tons of water back off the ramp without dumping the boat and the SEALs with it.

Except this water was anything but calm and she didn't dare slow down—this wave was moving with a serious attitude. She couldn't sink partway into the river, she didn't dare. She had to sink partway into the tidal bore wave itself.

She checked the rear view camera for a moment and saw the unbelievable: on the face of the boiling wave, a tiny rubber boat raced its engine and surfed down the face.

That's why pursuit had broken off, no one was stupid enough to mess with a tidal bore a hundred yards wide, two stories tall, and moving like a freight train. On the plus side, it would be assumed that anyone in a small boat would be dead. The river would be dredged and nothing would be found. So sorry.

Unless she screwed up and they found an entire American Special Operations helicopter at the bottom of the river.

The river twisted and turned her in sharp bends. The tidal bore crashed into one concrete-tiered bank and threw sheets of water thirty, forty, fifty feet into the air. And before it could slosh back down, another wave was reflecting off the other bank.

There was no neat standing wave here, there was only turbulent, muddy chaos.

She managed to plunge the ramp down into the water, but kept the nose of the *Carrie-Anne* held high so that her bird didn't drown.

Danielle was glad she couldn't afford another moment to look back because she'd wager that she wouldn't like what she saw.

"Six inches of water in the bay," Jason called over the intercom.

Danielle did her best to level out at that shallow depth. A foot would be better for the boat, but worse for the leading edge of the wave. Two feet would drown the Chinook and kill them all.

"Ten seconds," Jason called over the headset. She'd have to—

Another bridge loomed in her night vision. The support pilings were too close together and the bridge deck too low. She shot the nose up to dump the water load and climb over the bridge.

In the process, she released a small tidal wave of water out the back of the helo.

"Crap! Tell me I didn't sink them." A Zodiac didn't run well after a couple tons of water were dumped in it.

"No…but they won't need a shower for a long time."

Danielle cleared the bridge deck by inches and dove back down on the other side as the concrete river channel twisted left and narrowed.

"Now!" she shouted over the radio. There was another bridge less than a mile ahead. At this rate of speed, thirty seconds might be too long.

She got her tail in the water again.

"Six inches," Jason called. "A foot."

They needed the extra depth to make sure this worked.

"Five seconds."

It was going to be tight. She slowed down just a little bit.

The roar of the helo's engines was always loud inside the craft no matter how much sound insulation they installed. But now there was a new sound. A crashing of water, a twenty-foot high wall of surf in full breaking roar battering at her extended rear ramp.

The crew chief's curses told her plenty about the view.

"Two. One. Aboard!"

Danielle added lift. She wasn't subtle about it, she hauled up hard.

…and nothing happened.

The roar increased.

There were shouts, but there was no time to make sense of them.

The stern of the Chinook was slapped downward. They were in the wave.

If she couldn't shed water by climbing, maybe she could outrun it instead.

She aimed the nose down into the water to gain forward speed.

Water from the large cargo bay poured forward, washed about her feet, tried to tug them off the pedals. A small wave broke over the radios mounted on the flat console between the pilots' seats.

They shot past a giant golden ball of a building a dozen stories high. The Chinook and the gold ball would make a great photo if anyone was watching at four in the morning to take it. Though even if someone did, it would just look like a bad Photoshop job. A secret U.S. military helicopter—pitch black with no markings—surfing the tidal bore through the heart of a Chinese city. Like a 747 parked on an aircraft carrier, so not believable.

Danielle kept the nose down despite the cries over her headset. The bridge came closer and closer.

"Now!" Pete screamed beside her. "Pull up now!"

She waited another three seconds, gathering every knot of speed she could, and then tugged back hard, like popping a cork.

The *Carrie-Anne* stuck her nose in the air, going near vertical in her climb, and dumped water out the stern. She knew that the SEALs and all three of her crew would be desperately gripping the interior straps of the cargo bay so that they and their boat weren't washed back overboard with the outgoing flow.

There was a loud scraping sound as the Chinook dragged her belly plates over the bridge rail. Good thing the wheels were folded up or they'd have been ripped off.

Danielle dead-centered a streetlight which smashed Pete's side of the windscreen and then she was aloft. Hopefully the Chinese would discount the damage she caused as the result of tidal bore-tossed debris.

A hard bank to the left and she was once more driving back up into the Chinese hills as the tidal bore continued to spume and thrash its way up the Qiantang River.

Chapter 17

Pete had lost at least ten years of his life on that flight.

River water was still running aft, but now it was rivulets instead of a torrent.

"We all accounted for?" he called back over the intercom.

"Except for the shit from crapping my pants, we're all aboard," Jason reported from the rear ramp position.

"Pete," Luke pulled on a headset. "You're a dead man."

"Hey, it was my wave, but I wasn't the one flying."

"Danielle, you're a goddess. Pete, you're a dead man."

"No appreciation for—"

"Hey!" Danielle's complaint cut him off. "Could we get out of China first?"

"Oh, yeah," Pete needed to get his head back in the game. About a third of their electronics were cooked. "What's that smell?"

Luke made a foul spitting sound. "One of the most polluted rivers on the planet and the lady just dumped a thousand gallons of it on our heads."

They still had an intercom.

With a little fooling around, he managed to get a radio feed to Sophia off a military satellite. His direct radios linking him to the other helos and the Avenger were all offline.

"Have *Beatrix* wait for us offshore at," he read off the coordinates. "The Little Birds should turn back to the *Ashland*."

"They can't do that," Sophia reported. "Since they left the *Ashland* a Chinese patrol boat has been to harass her. They don't have enough fuel to reach Japan."

"How about the *Germantown?*" Pete tried to remember how fast it had been headed south and away from the area, but couldn't.

"No. Wait," he heard Sophia rattling some keys on her computer. "If you can order them to turn the ship and have it go north very fast, it should close the distance enough. I think. Maybe."

"Do it."

"They no listen to me," Sophia complained.

"Drop the Colonel's name. Drop the goddamn President's if you need to, but get them turned. And then order us an aerial tanker, we'll need to refuel both birds if we have to make it back to Japan on our own."

There was a brief pause, then Sophia giggled for a moment and was gone.

"What did that mean?" he asked Danielle.

"With a woman frohm Braazeel," she attempted an imitation of Sophia liquid tones, "You never weel nohh." Came out pretty well actually. "But don't be surprised if the President calls you about issuing orders in his name." Her normal light French accent sounded better.

"Our navs are fried. *Beatrix*, be ready to lead us out," but his mind wasn't really on the last order.

He opened his mouth to speak, to try and express some of what he was feeling for this woman beside him, when the radios and intercom disappeared in a cloud of sparks and circuit breakers began popping out all over the place.

Engines were still running, as was the night vision. They could still fly out of here, but the only way to communicate would be by shouting.

What he had to say would keep well enough until the next time they were alone together. For now, he focused on getting them home alive so that he'd have a chance to say it.

Chapter 18

As soon as they were off the C-5 transport jet at Mother Rucker, Alabama, they began reassembling their helos.

The SEALs did their "fade into the night" thing, but Danielle was sure she hadn't seen the last of them.

By midnight the helos were back together. They flew the three miles from Mother Rucker's main Cairns Airfield over to their hangar at Ech Stagefield in tight formation.

A small sign had been added above the entry door's code panel in their absence.

"The 5E," Danielle read aloud as the others gathered around her.

It was all the small brass plate said, but it was enough. It said this was home. She would get some other improvements made here: housing for the crew, convert the old Ech field offices into a training center, and other amenities. But what mattered now was that they had a home base. A place that they belonged.

The 5E tucked away their helos. The Avenger RPA, also reassembled after its journey in the C-5, was in a secure hangar at Cairns Airfield.

Not worried about further damage to the interior of the *Carrie-Anne*, Danielle had taken a fire hose to the interior back in Japan and washed the Hangzhou River out of her Chinook. Hopefully out of her life. She never wanted to try a stunt like that again.

Inside the hangar, a pallet of new electronics awaited them. Connie and Big John moved toward them as if drawn by irresistible magnets.

Danielle rested a hand on Connie's arm, "You just spent six hours reassembling a helicopter after flying all day from Japan. Tomorrow is soon enough."

She could feel the woman's conflict through their contact and then Connie laughed at herself.

"Yes," Sophia joined them. "Tomorrow we work, tonight we celebrate. That is good."

"Any suggestions?" Pete asked from close by her elbow. It didn't take a genius to know what kind of celebration he had in mind. But that was a celebration for just two. Danielle was looking forward to that as well, but this was a time for their whole team.

Everyone was looking to her, waiting for her to speak first. She scanned the faces of the 5E and resisted the alarm that wanted to surge through her. She had moved from being the outsider to becoming the core of the team. Danielle wasn't quite sure how that had happened. It was an honor beyond anything she deserved, so she'd have to figure out how to go about earning it…starting tomorrow.

For now, they still waited for her.

She had no idea of what to do next, and then she spotted the Frisbee in the Dozer's hand.

Danielle turned to challenge Pete The Rapier Napier but raised her voice to make sure everyone could hear.

"Everyone who isn't a complete loser…"

Pete just grinned.

"…grab a set of Night-Vision Goggles. It's time to play."

# # #

Pete stood on the unlit soccer field in the northeast corner of Fort Rucker. It was a typical Alabama early October night: heading from eighties to sixties beneath a sky so clear that it could be an inverted crystal bowl of stars.

And the NVGs amped that up about ten times, he never got used to the breathtaking splendor of the night sky, even if it was rendered in green and black.

Then he looked at the sign in front of him which showed the layout of the eighteen-hole disc golf course. Hole one was straight along the side of the soccer field to a steel pole. The upper half was a ring of light steel chains. If a Frisbee hit the chains, it would fall straight down into the waiting basket.

The goggles were heavy on his head, though far lighter than a helmet. Elastic straps over his head held it in place, the battery pack clipped to his belt. The mask covered half the upper half of his face and the dual lenses stuck out several inches like alien eyestalks.

They caused the nighttime world to be viewed in a combination of tunnel vision and brilliant apple green. The NVGs registered light and especially heat. Pete saw the crew shining brightly with their body heat, the ground less so, and the steel goals were a cool black in the night air.

He was getting to know the crew well enough to recognize them despite their faces being hidden behind NVGs.

Dozer the Mighty Quinn was distinctive for his size alone; he was also the keeper of the discs and was handing them out.

The DAP Hawks' pilots Julian and Rafe were a Mutt and Jeff duo even now fighting over who would get first toss.

Jason was as long and lean as his Chinook ramp gun.

Patty was by far the shortest one on the team, but could also be easily identified because she was always in the thick of it.

Sophia had amazing curves even in night-vision green.

Big John and Connie…they moved like a couple should. Not like his own parents, who got along well enough that he had far more happy memories of childhood than sad ones. Instead they fit together despite their physical disparity.

And then there was Danielle. He'd recognize her in a crowded room in pitch dark without NVGs; she was imprinted that deeply on his nervous system. As integrated as any helo had ever been. More so.

"Par three," Dozer said walking up to him. No, Dozer was walking up to Danielle. "But first, I need you to sign The Whistler." He held out the Frisbee with the hole shot through it and a marker pen.

Danielle reached out so tentatively to take it that he almost wondered if she'd refuse. Then she took a deep breath and signed it with a flourish.

She handed it off to Pete and he did the same.

When he went to return it to Dozer, he held up his hands palm out.

"Nope, we're playing teams. And I think you two should play with that disc."

Danielle's hesitation finally made sense.

When Pete had arrived to test the rookies, at least a lifetime ago, Danielle had stood to the side, outside the circle of the crew. Now she was no longer a loner, with no relations in the world except a long-gone father.

She now had a place in the world as clearly etched as any family.

Pete shook Dozer's hand in thanks. "You did it just right," he told the man. The big Alaskan actually bounced on the balls of his feet for a moment before looking up and grinning, the only part of his face that showed beneath the goggles.

"You guys go first," Dozer's voice was rough and he backed away quickly.

Pete handed the disc to Danielle, "Honor of the first toss, Spiderwoman."

That radiant smile was a gut punch even in a hundred shades of bright green.

The heat of their hands had left clear imprints on the disc that showed up easily in the NVGs. She cocked her arm and heaved the disc into the night.

Talk about a great way to spike the endgame ball. He missed Nicolai and the guys, but he wouldn't trade this team for the world.

A faint whistle sounded down the soccer field as his and Danielle's handprints spun around together.

# # #

At the thirteenth green, Danielle watched as Pete overshot the goal and the Frisbee flew out into the water hazard of the lake that defined the next three holes, it's little whistle sounding like a laugh right up to the moment of the splash.

Then he tried to make her go in and get it.

Danielle managed a quick twist and a well-planted shove that kept her dry and sent him stumbling waist deep into the water after the stray disc.

Laughter rang out from the other teams who were coming along behind them. Moments later Big John had to wade in after his own bad toss. Big John had immense strength, but Connie had all of the finesse.

Danielle and Pete both cleared the fourteenth without any problems, but it was her turn for the key toss on the fifteenth. It was either four throws to get around the end of the lake or one clean toss across the corner of it; a miss would definitely mean she was going swimming.

"What's it gonna be, Spiderwoman?"

"Stuff it, Napier," but she couldn't keep the joy out of her voice. The game had become a merry mayhem of calls up and down the line. Shouts of laughter. Sophia protesting after each toss that landed in the woods or a bush, saying that if this was a soccer ball she could beat them all to a pulp. Julian shoving Rafe into the lake because the man had stood too close to the shore; leaving both Julian and their shared disc dry.

"Need a better name for you than Spiderwoman," Pete whispered.

She'd been getting used to the name.

"Supergirl isn't enough. Sue Storm. Nope. How about Ripley?"

"From *Aliens?* Get a clue Napier. You're being cliché now."

"Am I?"

Danielle eyed the long toss once again. She could do it. The night was calm, only the slightest breath of air from the west. If she took off the goggles she knew the stars would be a warm carpet across the clear night sky rather than the cool one she saw now.

"Okay, how's this for not cliché," Pete's voice had changed. "Danielle?"

Something in his tone made her turn to look at him. His mouth, the only part of him that showed below the NVGs didn't have even the playful edge of a smile that she'd come to expect.

A slip of nerves echoed up her spine.

"What?"

"I love you."

That was it.

A bald, flat statement.

"You…" she couldn't even breathe.

"I thought a lot about what you said as we dove on the Hangzhou tidal bore. I never thought I could deserve a woman like you. But if you say you love me, I'd be pretty damn dumb to turn you away, wouldn't I?"

She nodded, but her head felt like it belonged to a bobble doll. She tried shaking it, but that felt equally strange.

"You…" she took another deep breath, "…love me? Just like that?"

"No, not just like that. I think it was from the moment you gave me sass about being one of the three Fates after I tried calling you the Hound of Hell. It seems you were right after all. You've snagged my thread, but good."

She searched for something to say, for some way to react. She looked down at her hands which ached with the tightness of her grip. She was holding The Whistler hard. Two patterns of bright green radiated outward from her hands where the plastic had been warmed by her grip. A small dark spot, where the bullet had punched through and left its mark. But whatever the past had done to it, the disc still flew true.

"Okay," Pete continued. "That didn't get quite the reaction I expected."

She looked back up at him still at a loss for what to say, but he turned away from her.

"Hey!" he shouted toward the others. "Members of the 5E. Gather around."

There was chattering and questions as everyone trotted over from their various positions among the closest few holes. When they were all gathered and asking what was up, he turned back to face her. A dozen green aliens with human mouths and mechanical eyes turned to face her.

"Now, let's try this," Pete peeled one of her hands off The Whistler and held it in both of his.

"Danielle Delacroix, our lady who guards the crossroads. I've done many dumb things, but let's see if I can do a really smart one instead. I'm going to risk doing this too soon, because I sure as hell don't want to be doing this too late."

Then he knelt down on one knee and the whispered conversations hushed.

"When you crossed my path, you gave me dreams to pursue. Now marry me and change my life. I swear on bended knee before these good people that I will do everything I can to deserve such a gift."

"And we'll kick his ass if he doesn't," Dozer spoke up and others laughed but murmured agreement.

Danielle considered all of the possible responses and exclamations and doubts.

She didn't need them.

She didn't need to think or to hesitate either. How many dreams-come-true knelt before her? So many she couldn't count them any more than the stars overhead.

But she couldn't just let him have her consent so easily, no matter how eager she was to give it.

"Well," she looked up at the rest of the 5E gathered close. At Sophia's clasped hands and shining smile. At how Connie and Big John were holding hands and leaning together with the shared memory of their moment. Now Danielle understood Connie's brief handclasp under the table, and just what was possible if you looked far enough outside the box to finally be able to see into its core.

"I'm going to say yes, but…" she let it trail. Everyone, including Pete, held their breath.

Then she looked down at his upturned face, or at least what she could see of it around the NVGs.

"But, it's my turn and I don't want to hold up the game."

She turned from the man she'd be sharing the rest of her life with and heaved The Whistler out into the dark. It shot over the lake toward the fifteenth pin with a little cry of joy that was the tiniest echo of the one in her heart.

About the Author

M. L. Buchman has over 30 novels in print. His military romantic suspense books have been nominated for the RT Reviewer's Choice of the Year award, and been named Barnes & Noble and NPR "Top 5 of the Year" and Booklist "Top 10 of the Year." In addition to romance, he also writes thrillers, fantasy, and science fiction.

In among his career as a corporate project manager he has: rebuilt and single-handed a fifty-foot sailboat, both flown and jumped out of airplanes, designed and built two houses, and bicycled solo around the world. He is now making his living as a full-time writer on the Oregon Coast with his beloved wife. He is constantly amazed at what you can do with a degree in Geophysics. You may keep up with his writing by subscribing to his newsletter at www.mlbuchman.com.

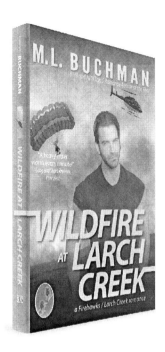

Wildfire at Larch Creek

a Firehawks / Larch Creek Novel

(excerpt)

T*wo-Tall Tim Harada leaned* over Akbar the Great's shoulder to look out the rear door of the DC-3 airplane.

"Ugly," he shouted over the roar of the engine and wind.

Akbar nodded rather than trying to speak.

Since ugly was their day job, it didn't bother Tim much, but this was worse than usual. It would be their fourth smokejump in nine days on the same fire. The Cottonwood Peak Fire was being a total pain in the butt, even worse than usual for a wildfire. Every time they blocked it in one direction, the swirling winds would turnabout and drive the fire toward a new point on the compass. Typical for the Siskiyou Mountains of northern California, but still a pain.

Akbar tossed out a pair of crepe paper streamers and they watched together. The foot-wide streamers caught wind and curled, loop-the-looped through vortices, and reversed direction at least three times. Pretty much the worst conditions possible for a parachute jump.

"It's what we live for!"

Akbar nodded and Tim didn't have to see his best friend's face to know about the fierce wildness of his white grin on his Indian-dark face. Or the matching one against his own part-Vietnamese coloring. Many women told him that his mixed Viet, French-Canadian, and Oklahoman blood made him intriguingly exotic—a fact that had never hurt his prospects in the bar.

The two of them were the first-stick smokejumpers for Mount Hood Aviation, the best freelance firefighters of them all. This was—however moronic—*precisely* what they lived for. He'd followed Akbar the Great's lead for five years and the two of them had climbed right to the top.

"Race you," Akbar shouted then got on the radio and called directions about the best line of attack to "DC"—who earned his nickname from his initials matching the DC-3 jump plane he piloted.

Tim moved to give the deployment plan to the other five sticks still waiting on their seats; no need to double check it with Akbar, the best approach was obvious. Heck, this was the top crew. The other smokies barely needed the briefing; they'd all been watching through their windows as the streamers cavorted in the chaotic winds.

Then, while DC turned to pass back over the jump zone, he and Akbar checked each others' gear. Hard hat with heavy mesh face shield, Nomex fire suit tight at the throat, cinched at the waist, and tucked in the boots. Parachute and reserve properly buckled, with the static line clipped to the wire above the DC-3's jump door. Pulaski fire axe, fire shelter, personal gear bag, chain saw on a long rope tether, gas can…the list went on, and through long practice took them under ten seconds to verify.

Five years they'd been jumping together, the last two as lead stick. Tim's body ached, his head swam with fatigue, and he was already hungry though they'd just eaten a full meal at base camp and a couple energy bars on the short flight back to the fire. All the symptoms were typical for a long fire.

DC called them on close approach. Once more Akbar leaned out the door, staying low enough for Tim to lean out over him. Not too tough as Akbar was a total shrimp and Tim had earned the "Two-Tall" nickname for being two Akbars tall. He wasn't called Akbar the Great for his height, but rather for his powerful build and unstoppable energy on the fire line.

"Let's get it done and…" Tim shouted in Akbar's ear as they approached the jump point.

"…come home to Mama!" and Akbar was gone.

Tim actually hesitated before launching himself after Akbar and ended up a hundred yards behind him.

Come home to Mama? Akbar had always finished the line, *Go get the girls.* Ever since the wedding, Akbar had gotten all weird in the head. Just because he was married and happy was no excuse to—

The static line yanked his chute. He dropped below the tail of the DC-3—always felt as if he had to duck, but doorways on the ground did the same thing to him—and the chute caught air and jerked him hard in the groin.

The smoke washed across the sky. High, thin cirrus clouds promised an incoming weather change, but wasn't going to help them much today. The sun was still pounding the wilderness below with a scorching, desiccating heat that turned trees into firebrands at a single spark.

The Cottonwood Peak Fire was chewing across some hellacious terrain. Hillsides so steep that some places you needed mountaineering gear to go chase the flames. Hundred-and-fifty foot Doug firs popping off like fireworks. Ninety-six thousand acres, seventy percent contained and a fire as angry as could be that they were beating it down.

Tim yanked on the parachute's control lines as the winds caught him and tried to fling him back upward into the sky. On a jump like this you spent as much time making sure that the chute didn't tangle with itself in the chaotic winds as you did trying to land somewhere reasonable.

Akbar had called it right though. They had to hit high on this ridge and hold it. If not, that uncontained thirty percent of the wildfire was going to light up a whole new valley to the east and the residents of Hornbrook, California were going to have a really bad day.

His chute spun him around to face west toward the heart of the blaze. Whoever had rated this as seventy percent contained clearly needed his head examined. Whole hillsides were still alight with flame. It was only because the MHA smokies had cut so many firebreaks over the last eight days, combined with the constant pounding of the big Firehawk helicopters dumping retardant loads every which way, that the whole mountain range wasn't on fire.

Tim spotted Akbar. Below and to the north. Damn but that guy could fly a chute. Tim dove hard after him.

Come home to Mama! Yeesh! But the dog had also found the perfect lady. Laura Jenson: wilderness guide, expert horse-woman—who was still trying to get Tim up on one of her beasts—and who was really good for Akbar. But it was as if Tim no longer recognized his best friend.

They used to crawl out of a fire, sack out in the bunks for sixteen-straight, then go hit the bars. *What do I do for a living? I parachute out of airplanes to fight wildfires by hand.* It wowed the women every time, gained them pick of the crop.

Now when Akbar hit the ground, Laura would be waiting in her truck and they'd disappear to her little cabin in the woods. What was up with that anyway?

Tim looked down and cursed. He should have been paying more attention. Akbar was headed right into the center of the only decent clearing, and Tim was on the verge of overflying the ridge and landing in the next county.

He yanked hard on the right control of his chute, swung in a wide arc, and prayed that the wind gods would be favorable just this once. They were, by inches. Instead of smacking face first into the drooping top of a hemlock that he hadn't seen coming, he swirled around it, receiving only a breath-stealing slap to the ribs, and dropped in close beside Akbar.

"Akbar the Great rules!"

His friend demanded a high five for making a cleaner landing than Tim's before he began stuffing away his chute.

In two minutes, the chutes were in their stuff bags and they'd shifted over to firefighting mode. The next two sticks dropped into the space they'd just vacated. Krista nailed her landing more cleanly than Tim or Akbar had. Jackson ate an aspen, but it was only a little one, so he was on the ground just fine, but he had to cut down the tree to recover his chute. Didn't matter; they had to clear the whole ridge anyway—except everyone now had an excuse to tease him.

# # #

Forty hours later Tim had spent thirty hours non-stop on the line and ten crashed face first into his bunk. Those first thirty had been a grueling battle of clearing the ridgeline and scraping the earth down to mineral soils. The heat had been obscene as the fire climbed the face of the ridge, rising until it had towered over them in a wall of raging orange and thick, smoke-swirl black a couple dozen stories high.

The glossy black-and-racing-flame painted dots of the MHA Firehawks had looked insignificant as they dove, dropping eight tons of bright-red retardant alongside the fire or a thousand gallons of water directly on the flames as called for. The smaller

MD500s were on near-continuous call-up to douse hotspots where sparks had jumped the line. Emily, Jeannie, and Vern, their three night-drop certified pilots, had flown right through the night to help them kill it. Mickey and the others picking it back up at daybreak.

Twice they'd been within minutes of having to run and once they were within seconds of deploying their fire shelters, but they'd managed to beat it back each time. There was a reason that smokejumpers were called on a Type I wildfire incident. They delivered. And the Mount Hood Aviation smokies had a reputation of being the best in the business; they'd delivered on that as well.

Tim had hammered face down into his bunk, too damn exhausted to shower first. Which meant his sheets were now char-smeared and he'd have to do a load of laundry. He jumped down out of the top bunk, shifting sideways to not land on Akbar if he swung out of the lower bunk at the same moment…except he wasn't there. His sheets were neat and clean, the blanket tucked in. Tim's were the only set of boots on the tiny bit of floor the two of them usually jostled for. Akbar now stayed overnight in the bunkhouse only if Laura was out on a wilderness tour ride with her horses.

Tim thought about swapping his sheets for Akbar's clean ones, but it hardly seemed worth the effort.

Following tradition, Tim went down the hall, kicking the doors and receiving back curses from the crashed-out smokies. The MHA base camp had been a summer camp for Boy Scouts or something way too many years ago. The halls were narrow and the doors thin.

"Doghouse!" he hollered as he went. He raised a fist to pound on Krista's door when a voice shouted from behind it.

"You do that, Harada, and I'm gonna squish your tall ass down to Akbar's runt size."

That was of course a challenge and he beat on her door with a quick rattle of both fists before sprinting for the safety of the men's showers.

Relative safety.

He was all soaped up in the doorless plywood shower stall, when a bucket of ice-cold water blasted him back against the wall.

He yelped! He couldn't help himself. She must have dipped it from the glacier-fed stream that ran behind the camp it was so freaking cold.

Her raucous laugh said that maybe she had.

He considered that turnabout might be fair play, but with Krista you never knew. If he hooked up a one-and-a-half inch fire hose, she might get even with a three hundred-gallon helicopter drop. And then… Maybe he'd just shame her into buying the first round at the Doghouse Inn.

Tim resoaped and scrubbed and knew he'd still missed some patches of black. The steel sheets attached to the wall as mirrors were as useless now as they'd been before decades of Boy Scouts had tried to carve their initials into them. Usually he and Akbar checked each other because you ended up with smoke or char stains in the strangest spots.

But Akbar wasn't here.

Tim didn't dare wait for any of the others. If he was caught still in the shower by all the folks he'd just rousted from their sacks, it wouldn't turn out well.

He made it back to his room in one piece. The guys who'd showered last night were already on their way out. Good, they'd grab the table before he got down into town and hit the Doghouse Inn. The grimy ones weren't moving very fast yet.

Tim had slept through breakfast and after the extreme workout of a long fire his stomach was being pretty grouchy about that.

# # #

As Macy Tyler prepared for it, she regretted saying yes to a date with Brett Harrison. She regretted not breaking the date the second after she'd made it. And she hoped that by the time the evening with Brett Harrison was over she wouldn't regret not dying of some exotic Peruvian parrot flu earlier in the day.

Just because they'd both lived in Larch Creek, Alaska their entire lives was not reason enough for her to totally come apart. Was it?

Actually it was nothing against Brett particularly. But she knew she was still borderline psychotic about men. It was her first date since punching out her fiancé on the altar, and the intervening six months had not been sufficient for her to be completely rational on the subject.

After fussing for fifteen minutes, she gave herself up as a lost cause. Macy hanked her dark, dead straight, can't-do-crap-with-it hair back in a long ponytail, put on a bra just because—it was mostly optional with her build, and pulled on a t-shirt. Headed for the door, she caught sight of herself in the hall mirror and saw which t-shirt she'd grabbed: *Helicopter Pilots Get It Up Faster.*

She raced back to her bedroom and switched it out for: *People Fly Airplanes, Pilots Fly Helicopters.* And knocked apart her ponytail in the process. Hearing Brett's pickup on the gravel street, she left her hair down, grabbed a denim jacket, and headed for the door.

Macy hurried out and didn't give Brett time to climb down and open the door of his rattletrap Ford truck for her, if he'd even thought of it.

"Look nice, Macy," was all the greeting he managed which made her feel a little better about the state of her own nerves.

He drove into town, which was actually a bit ridiculous, but he'd insisted he would pick her up. Town was four blocks long and she only lived six blocks from the center of it. They rolled down Buck Street, up Spitz Lane, and down Dave Court to Jack London Avenue—which had the grandest name but was only two blocks long because of a washout at one end and the back of the pharmacy-gas station at the other.

This north side of town was simply "The Call" because all of the streets were named for characters from *The Call of the Wild.*

French Pete and Jack London had sailed the Alaskan seaways together. So, as streets were added, the founders had made sure they were named after various of London's books. Those who lived in "The Fang" to the south were stuck with characters from *White Fang* for their addresses including: Grey Beaver Boulevard, Weedon Way, and Lip-lip Lane.

Macy wished that she and French Pete's mate Hilma—he went on to marry an Englishwoman long after he'd left and probably forgotten Larch Creek—hadn't been separated by a century of time; the woman must have really been something.

Macy tried to start a conversation with Brett, but rapidly discovered that she'd forgotten to bring her brain along on this date and couldn't think of a thing to say.

They hit the main street at the foot of Hal's Folly—the street was only the length of the gas station, named for the idiot who drove a dogsled over thin ice and died for it in London's book. It was pure irony that the street was short and steep. When it was icy, the Folly could send you shooting across the town's main street and off into Larch Creek—which was much more of a river than a creek. The street froze in early October, but the river was active enough that you didn't want to go skidding out onto the ice before mid-November.

Brett drove them up past the contradictory storefronts which were all on the "high side" of the road—the "low side" and occasionally the road itself disappeared for a time during the spring floods. The problem was that almost all of the buildings were from the turn of the century, but half were from the turn of this century and half were from the turn before. The town had languished during the 1900s and only experienced a rebirth over the last four decades.

Old log cabins and modern stick-framed buildings with generous windows stood side by side. Mason's Galleria was an ultramodern building of oddly-shaded glass and no right angles. One of the town mysteries was how Mason kept the art gallery in business when Larch Creek attracted so few tourists. Macy's favorite suggestion was that the woman—who was always dressed in the sharpest New York clothes and spoke so fast that no one could understand her—was actually a front for the Alaskan mafia come to rule Larch Creek.

This newest, most modern building in town was tight beside the oldest and darkest structure.

French Pete's, where Brett parked his truck, was the anchor at the center of town and glowered out at all of the other structures. The heavy-log, two-story building dominated Parisian Way—as the main street of Larch Creek was named by the crazy French prospector who founded the town in the late-1800s. He'd named the trading post after himself and the town after the distinctive trees that painted the surrounding hills yellow every fall. French Pete had moved on, but a Tlingit woman he'd brought with him stayed and bore him a son after his departure. It was Hilma who had made sure the town thrived.

There had been a recent upstart movement to rename the town because having the town of Larch Creek *on* Larch Creek kept confusing things. "Rive Gauche" was the current favorite during heavy drinking at French Pete's because the town was on the "left bank" of Larch Creek. If you were driving in on the only road, the whole town was on the left bank; like the heart of Paris. The change had never made it past the drinking stage, so most folk just ignored the whole topic, but it persisted on late Saturday nights.

Macy took strength from the town. She had loved it since her first memories. And just because she'd been dumb enough to agree to a date with Brett, she wasn't going to blame Larch Creek for that.

Well, not much. Perhaps, if there were more than five hundred folk this side of Liga Pass, there would be a single man that she could date who didn't know every detail of her life. She still clung onto the idea that she'd find a decent man somewhere among the chaff.

Dreamer!

That wasn't entirely fair. After all, some of them, like Brett, were decent enough.

The problem was that she, in turn, knew every detail of their lives. Macy had gone to school with each of them for too many years and knew them all too well. A lot of her classmates left at a dead run after graduation and were now up in Fairbanks, though very few went further afield. The thirty-mile trip back to Larch Creek from "the city" might as well be three hundred for how often they visited. The first half of the trip was on Interstate 4 which was kept open year round. But once you left the main highway, the road narrowed and twisted ten miles over Liga Pass with harsh hairpins and little forgiveness. It didn't help that it was closed as often as it was open in the winter months. The last five miles were through the valley's broad bottom land.

The town was four blocks long from the Unitarian church, which was still a movie theater on Friday and Saturday nights, at the north end of town to the grange at the south end. The houses crawled up the hills to the east. And the west side of the fast-running, glacier-fed river, where the forested hills rose in an abrupt escarpment, belonged to bear, elk, and wolf. Only Old Man Parker had a place on that side, unable to cross during fall freeze-up or spring melt-out. But he and his girlfriend didn't come into town much even when the way was open across running water or thick ice.

The main road ran north to meet the highway to Fairbanks, and in the other direction ended five miles south at Tena. Tena simply meant "trail" in the Tanana dialect and added another couple dozen families to the area. The foot trail out of Tena lead straight toward the massif of Denali's twenty-thousand foot peak which made the valley into a picture postcard.

Macy did her best to draw strength from the valley and mountain during the short drive to French Pete's. Once they hit Parisian Way, a bit of her brain returned. She even managed a polite inquiry about Brett's construction business and was pretty pleased at having done so. Thankfully they were close, so his answer was kept brief.

"Mostly it's about shoring up people's homes before winter hits. There are only a couple new homes a year and Danny gets most of those." He sounded bitter, it was a rivalry that went back to the senior prom and Cheryl Dahl, the prettiest Tanana girl in town.

The fact that Brett and Danny drank together most Saturdays and Cheryl had married Mike Nichol—the one she'd accompanied to the prom—and had three equally beautiful children in Anchorage had done nothing to ease their epic rivalry.

Or perhaps it was because Brett's blue pickup had a bumper sticker that said *America Is Under Construction* and Danny's blue truck had a drawing of his blue bulldozer that read *Vogon Constructor Fleet—specialist in BIG jobs.*

"Small towns," Macy said in the best sympathetic tone she could muster. It was difficult to not laugh in his face, because it was *so* small-town of them.

"This place looks wackier every time," they'd stopped in front of French Pete's. "Carl has definitely changed something, just can't pick it out."

Macy looked up in surprise. The combined bar and restaurant appeared no different to her. Big dark logs made a structure two-stories high with a steep roof to shed the snow. A half dozen broad steps led up to a deep porch that had no room for humans; it was jammed with Carl Deville's collection of "stuff."

"Your junk. My stuff," Carl would always say when teased about it by some unwary tourist. After such an unthinking comment, they were then as likely to find horseradish in their turkey sandwich as not.

There was the broken Iditarod sled from Vic Hornbeck's failed race bid in the late 1970s piled high with dropped elk antlers. An Elks Lodge hat from Poughkeepsie, New York still hung over one handle of the sled. The vintage motorcycle of the guy who had come through on his way to solo climb up Denali from the north along Muldrow Glacier and descend to the south by Cassin Ridge was still there, buried under eleven years of detritus. Whether he made the crossing and didn't come back or died on the mountain, no one ever knew.

"Man asked me to hold it for him a bit," Carl would offer in his deep laconic style when asked by some local teen who lusted after the wheels. "Don't see no need to hustle it out from under him. 'Sides, the baby girl he left in Carol Swenson's belly whilst he was here is ten now. Mayhaps she'll want it at sixteen."

There was an old wooden lobster pot—that Macy had never understood because the Gulf of Alaska to the south wasn't all that much closer than the Beaufort Sea to the north and the pot looked like it was from Maine—with a garden gnome-sized bare-breasted hula dancer standing inside it; her ceramic paint worn to a patina by too many Alaskan winters spent topless and out of doors. A hundred other objects were scattered about including worn-out gold panning equipment, a couple of plastic river kayaks with "For Rent" signs that might have once been green and sky blue before the sun leached out all color—though she'd never seen them move. And propped in the corner was the wooden propeller from Macy's first plane that she'd snapped when her wheel had caught in an early hole in the permafrost up near Nenana. That was before she'd switched to helicopters. She'd spent a week there before someone could fly in a replacement.

"Looks the same to me."

Brett eyed her strangely as he held open the door.

And just like that she knew she'd blown what little hope this date had right out of the water. Brett had been trying to make conversation and she'd done her true-false test. It wasn't like she was anal, it was more like everyone simply treated her as if she was.

Inside was dark, warm, and just as cluttered. A century or more of oddbits had been tacked to the walls: old photos, snowshoes strung with elk hide, a rusted circular blade several feet across from the old sawmill that had closed back in the sixties, and endless other bits and pieces that Carl and his predecessors had gathered. He claimed direct lineage back to French Pete Deville, through Hilma. It wasn't hard to believe; Carl looked like he'd been born behind the bar. Looked like he might die there too.

The fiction section of the town library lined one long wall of French Pete's. Most of the non-fiction was down at the general store except for religion, movies, and anything to do with mechanics. They were down in the movie house-church's lobby, the mechanical guides because the pharmacy-gas station was next door.

Though Carl didn't have any kin, Natalie, the ten-year-old daughter of Carol Swenson and the mountain climber with the left-behind motorcycle, was sitting up on a high barstool playing chess against Carl. It was a place she could be found most days when there wasn't school and Carol was busy over at the general store and post office. She was such a fixture that over the last few years everyone had pretty much come to expect Natty to take over French Pete's someday.

Macy scanned the tables hoping that no one would recognize her, fat chance in a community the size of Larch Creek.

And then she spotted the big table back in the corner beneath the moose-antler chandelier. It was packed.

Oh crap! She'd forgotten it was Sunday.

Too late to run for cover, she guided Brett in the other direction to a table in the corner. She managed to sit with her back to her father's expression of mock horror. That she could deal with.

But it would have been easier if Mom hadn't offered a smile and a wink.

Available now.

For more information on this and other titles,
please visit www.mlbuchman.com

Other works by this author:

Romances

-The Night Stalkers-
The Night Is Mine
I Own the Dawn
Daniel's Christmas
Wait Until Dark
Frank's Independence Day
Peter's Christmas
Take Over at Midnight
The Night Stalkers Special
Features
Light Up the Night
Chistmas at Steel Beach
Bring On the Dusk

-The Night Stalkers 5E-
Target of the Heart

-Firehawks-
Pure Heat
Wildfire at Dawn
Full Blaze
Wildfire at Larch Creek

-Angelo's Hearth-
Where Dreams Are Born
Where Dreams Reside
Maria's Christmas Table
Where Dreams Unfold
Where Dreams Are Written

Thrillers

Swap Out!
One Chef!
Two Chef!

SF/F

Nara
Monk's Maze

-Dieties Anonymous-
Cookbook from Hell: Reheated
Saviors 101: the first book of
the Reluctant Messiah